The Ballad of
T. RANTULA

By Kit Reed

The Ballad of
T. RANTULA

a novel by **Kit Reed**

Little, Brown and Company   Boston   Toronto

FIRST EDITION
T 05/79

Library of Congress Cataloging in Publication Data

Reed, Kit.
    The ballad of T. Rantula.

    I. Title.
PZ4.R3245Bal [PS3568.E367]   813'.5'4   78-20975
ISBN 0-316-73660-0

Designed by D. Christine Benders
Published simultaneously in Canada
by Little, Brown & Company (Canada) Limited
PRINTED IN THE UNITED STATES OF AMERICA

for Liz and Pat with love

The Ballad of
T. RANTULA

1.

SO WE GOT MY MOTHER back. At least I think we did. Pop and I had to go around to a lot of different places before we could get her to listen to us and after that we had to find the right things to say to her. Here we are all three together again after all, a little sore in spots but together, at least for now, and we wouldn't be if it hadn't been for Tig, or what happened to Tig.

We were so dumb when she left, we wasted a lot of time being civilized and what is it, understanding, trying to adjust. Pop bumped into things a lot, he had a face like a scraped knee—pale, blank, just about to bleed. He was always more or less surprised to see me, surprised he had lost her, surprised.

Um.

Uh.

What

What happened

What?

I'm only the kid, Pop. How am I supposed to know?

I didn't even know about Tig.

Maybe we both belong up there on the hill with the rest of the re-tards, making baskets and stringing beads. I could admire Pop's potholders and he could help me with the pine needle pillows and they would give him something to smooth off the parts that hurt, uppers with his oatmeal, downers in the orange juice, they would never let him teach college if they saw that dip-faced look creeping over him. Pop knows more stuff about a lot of little things than anybody I've ever met, but he couldn't figure out what happened, what to do. The smartest people in the world come to the college where he teaches, imagine all those parents paying thirty thousand bucks so their kids can learn things from—our fathers. Right, they are geniuses, except: surprise every-body, this is a secret, they don't know *anything*. They have read zillions of books and enough newspapers to burn down the Big Pru, they have been to more lectures than the City of Boston put together, they have written enough books to stuff five dozen bookmobiles and be-tween them they still can't figure out the simplest little things: what's happening, how to behave.

Pop would stumble into some room where I was read-ing with his face wide open and full of questions.

I would hang onto my book, scared to death he was going to ask.

He knew I didn't know either, so finally he would say, *This isn't what it used to be like.*

So I could say, *What what used to be like?*

Being a kid. He would look at my book: Zen secrets? Kesey? Freud? *Dammit, Fred, why don't you ever play outside?*

Pop, it's two below.

Fred, he would say, *we spent half our time on the river, we had this old boat, once we stayed out overnight and my folks called the police.*

Once Tig and I hitched to Cambridge, we slept in the movies and when we got home the next day there wasn't anybody either place. Tig's Mom thought he was at my house and Pop thought I was at Tig's. Besides, nobody calls me Fred.

Blue herons, Fred. Double-crested cormorants. Maybe we ought to get you a boat. He put his mother's name in the middle of mine: Frederick Futch Crandall. *Are you listening?*

My real friends call me Futch. *Pop, it's winter, and besides.* If you dropped a match on our river the whole thing would go up.

Right, Fred. This isn't Florida.

Neither is Florida any more. The one time we went down there it was all Colonel Chicken and old ladies with wrinkled brown middles, Ronald McDonald in one big parking lot.

Oh Fred, what happened to your childhood?

What do you mean, Pop? This is it.

He didn't have any answers so he would cut his eyes at me, in hopes.

I didn't have them either, I never knew any. I didn't

even know what was happening to Tig. When something is over you can see what was going on at the time, what you might have done about it, it's like watching those old movies about the assassinations: any fool can see what's coming because we know how it came out, but my father says when they shot President Kennedy everybody was surprised.

Now Mom is back in the act, with her face scrubbed shiny in the middle of all that blown brown hair, she looks like a surprised flower. Her hands are floating; she hasn't figured out what to do with them. She tries to fold her long arms around me. *Well, Freddy, here we are. What do you want me to . . .*

I know what she's trying to do. She comes up behind me when I'm not looking and hugs me a lot, hanging on; they sit around planning things I don't want.

One thing is they are going to make a big deal out of Christmas on account of forgetting my birthday in the summer. She phoned in from somewhere around six when I had already given up and then Pop took me to Howard Johnson's like he had been planning it, I had the dollar-fifty split but when he tried to put the fourteen candles in the whipped cream on the top I told him to forget it, afterward he wrote a fifty-dollar check.

Last Christmas I got everything I wanted and the day after, I went over to Tig's because Mom and Pop were having a fight. It was nothing special, just your standard usual, but they don't like you to see them because later on they can pretend it never happened; if you're around they can see you remembering and it makes them mad. Nobody ever fights at Tig's house because they are either never around or if they are around they're sleeping it off, you either tiptoe and whisper or else freeze your butt on the doorstep because they will kill anybody that wakes them up.

Tig was outside in Mr. Tilghman's brand new pigskin riding boots, he had stuffed his jeans into them and I could see the water marks where the snow had melted and soaked in. He had his mother's ski poles and he was stamping out some kind of pattern with them, he didn't even see me at first.

I said, "Hey, Tig."

I thought he would come over to the fence but he just stood there in the middle of this design he was making and ducked his head like a little kid. He and Welles and I have been together for as long as I can remember but all last year, when Welles and I were changing and knew it, Tig was busy doing something else.

I came around the fence to look at the stampings in the snow, it was a little bit like a giant snowflake, geometric. From the looks of it he had already been there for a couple of hours and he was only making it deeper, not doing anything new. I said, "Whudju get?"

"Watch *out*."

"I got a digital watch."

"I said, watch *out*. You're stepping on it."

"I am not." I wasn't anywhere near his damn pattern, I was just walking around the outside of it, trying to figure out how he had gotten in the middle because there weren't any footprints leading in. He must have filled them in after him, because it looked like there was no way in and no way out. "You want to play records or something?"

"I don't know." He was looking at his stupid lace-work, trying to find some way to get out without spoiling it.

"Are you going to talk to me or not?"

"Watch out, you're going to wreck it."

"What are you gonna do, fly out?"

He just shrugged, looking trapped.

"Maybe you could levitate."

"Shut up."

"Well you can't stay there forever."

"Go to hell."

"What if you took off the boots?"

He started to explain, "I can't do that without moving my feet, but maybe . . ." then he saw I was making fun of him and he said, "Why don't you just go away?"

"Because you're being stupid." I started tramping around in a circle around *his* circle, I could see him getting madder and madder because he was scared to death I was going to step on it, I kept making these assy suggestions, "We could spray it with plaster of Paris so it would keep, or else you could stay in there and freeze to death, but whatever you do, be sure you die standing up."

Every time I would say anything he would yell "Shut up," finally he yelled, "Shut up, faggot."

"Don't say that again or I'll jump in it."

"Faggot."

"I'm warning you."

He was weaving in place, I got closer and closer to the edge of his stupid pattern, I think my toe slipped. He really wanted to come out and hit me but he was still stuck in his picture so he threw a ski pole instead.

"Missed me, missed me, now you got to kiss me." I accidentally kicked some snow on part of it.

Then he swung the other pole but he lost his balance and before he knew what he was doing he had lunged a couple of steps trying to get it back, the pattern was wrecked and he was out. He grabbed me and we wrestled in the snow, usually when we do that we end up laughing but neither of us felt like it, I had to let him rub snow in my face so we could be even and then he let me up.

I said, "What was that crap?"

His hands and elbows went flying. "I don't know."

"I mean, what's the matter?"

"Nothing." His face was a crooked triangle; he was trying to grin. "You know."

Something about the parents. We had to get off it quick. "I got the big astrology book, the one that has the charts. My grandmother got me more dumb Hardy Boys, she is so scared I'm going to read something that will make me sick. Whudju get?"

Tig shrugged. "Oh, you know."

"You know what we did yesterday, after the turkey? We went to the movies." Part of my stomach was jumping because I could still hear the folks the way I left them: sawing back and forth. "A double feature and we had supper at McDonald's because nobody could stand to look the turkey in the face."

"You know what he gave my mother?" Tig had this funny, intent expression because that's all he ever has to add up: what they got.

"No, what."

"Matching amethysts. And Chanel."

He looked so depressed I said, "Oh, wow."

"And a fur hat, she got him a fur-lined raincoat and these riding boots."

"Mine got each other sweaters and books, again."

"Yeah, well." He was looking better. "OK, here's what I got."

"A sock full of switches."

"A whole lot of crap. They got me Head skis with the boots, I got about eight board games and a calculator and my big present . . ." He looked embarrassed but he had to go on listing the presents and I had to keep going, Wow, or, Great, because as long as we could do that we could pretend they really added up. "My big present was this Space Walk set, it's mechanical with planets that light up."

I said the only thing I could say: "Gee, Tig, you always get the best things."

At least that part is true.

Tig always gets the most, whole electric railroads before he was big enough to play with them and Rock'em Sock'em Robots, when they left him with his grandmother that one Christmas they brought back a toy chair lift with electrical people that he and Welles and I broke the first day, we were in the first grade and Mr. Tilghman got so mad we didn't go back to Tig's house for nearly a month. He had the scale model fortress and the electric hockey game, year before last it was the Skeanateles electric road racing set, we were twelve by that time, which is maybe too old? The funny thing is we get older and bigger but the toys seem to stay the same: flashy little kid things, not to keep Tig little but to prove something that they aren't sure of any more than Tig, they can all three point to the toy that cost so much money and say, See. Last year it was the Space Walk and this year, I don't know, maybe they were going to get him a bicycle pump to blow himself back

up with, or else some Kleenex to stuff his cheeks with
to make him look more natural.

I had to see the Space Walk so we went in through the
kitchen, I thought I heard Tig's mother upstairs but we
slipped right down the basement steps. We liked to hang
out over there because nobody ever bothers us, I told
Mom that once when we were having a fight, she hit me
on the ear and said, "That's because nobody gives a
damn." In a way it might be worth it, at least I used to
think so.

The basement is full of Tig's stuff: the fire truck and
his hobby horse with the real tail and all his baby books
and stuffed animals. They had put the Space Walk on
the Ping-Pong table, so we couldn't play, and the worst
thing was it didn't work.

"It's a bummer," Tig said, and plugged it in.

For a minute it was beautiful. The planets all lit up.
There was a whole plastic landscape with craters and
rocks with this tower in the middle where the motor
was, it had all the planets and moons and command
modules coming out on rods and a big phony sun on top.
I said, "Is that all it does?"

"We can't get it to work."

"Of course you can get it to work." I pushed Tig's
hand out of the way and threw the switch. For one
minute the thing whirred and I thought the planets were
going to start and then it went out.

Tig said, "See, I told you."

"You mean you've got this great big expensive present
and it doesn't even work?"

Tig said, "We could do something else."

"I don't want to do anything else." Why was I so
mad? I don't know if it was my folks or the snow pat-

tern or the amethysts or what. "Let's get your father to fix it."

"We can't, he's asleep."

I don't know why I couldn't quit. "He gave it to you, he ought to make it work."

"Forget it."

"What kind of a present is that?"

"We were up half the night trying to get it going," Tig said. "Dad took the whole thing apart, he even called this engineer he knows."

"Bullshit."

"No kidding." Tig and I both knew he was lying. "He tried to get it working, it was almost morning when we quit, that's why he's still asleep."

If he hadn't lied maybe I could have let him off, but I had to say, "Why don't you see if he's awake?"

"Leave me alone."

"All you have to do is check."

"I'm not going to bother him."

I knew what I was doing, I said the one thing he couldn't let go by. "He wouldn't fix it if you did."

"Damn you, Futch. Damn you to hell." Tig was going up the basement stairs.

"What are you doing?"

"Going to get him, what do you think?"

(The last time we got that mad it was Tig at me, for insisting there was a Santa Claus, I think we were six.) I said, "All right, smartass, go and get him, I'll sit here and wait."

"Don't go way." He reached inside the kitchen where the switch was and turned off the playroom light.

I felt rotten, sitting there in the dark, I wanted to kill him for being stupid and I wanted to kill his damn dumb father that gave expensive presents and wouldn't even set them up. Sooner or later Tig was going to have to give up and come back down here and admit he was being dumb. If I could get him to quit lying it would serve him right. No. It would be for his own good. If he would just admit it then we could clear out and do something else. I waited a long time. I found a flashlight and read a couple of comics and he didn't come. Then I thought maybe I ought to sneak out and go home, when he came back with whatever lie he was making up I would be gone, he could stand there in front of his expensive present and see how stupid he had been.

So I sneaked up the basement steps and listened at the door. It was quiet so I tried the knob; from where I was standing I couldn't see anybody, so I came up into the kitchen and there was Tig, he didn't even look up. He was sitting at the table in the middle of yesterday's leftovers, they had left the turkey carcass out and there were a couple of mungy-looking pies plus a whole box of candy that somebody had opened but nothing had been touched; as far as I could tell Tig hadn't eaten anything, he hadn't even moved. He didn't seem to notice me, I was still trying to figure out what to say, whether to make a joke or apologize or whether I should make him be the one to start; then he got a funny look, he had tuned out but he was listening for something and now I heard it; somebody was coming down the stairs. Tig's hands went spastic, trying to do eight things at once, and he was dragging another chair over and pushing me into it so we could face whoever it was that was coming barefooted. He wanted us to look happy, interrupted: See, we were only having lunch.

It was Tig's father, he was still in his bathrobe with

nothing underneath. He goes around like that and I think he wants you to see him but I don't know for sure because when he sits down and the robe slides I will never look. He is so handsome he gives me the creeps; Pop has a crooked face, he is funny-looking in a way that makes you want to smile, which is what makes him look like my father and nobody else. Everybody's father has something of his own, a mess of wrinkles or a bumpy nose or extra chins, something, but Mr. Tilghman is so handsome he doesn't look like anybody at all. From his face you would think he never did anything, even lose his temper, or anything he did do, he erased.

He went to the stove without even noticing and poured some coffee. While he drank it he looked more or less over our heads at the snow on the kitchen windowframe.

Tig and I just sat there, um, uh, um.

His father stood there looking like a great big store dummy. Tig's hands were flying and his mouth was all squinched up, I couldn't stand it, I thought if I said something maybe we could get it over with.

"Hi Mr. Tilghman."

"Oh, Fred." I guess it was too bad I said anything, now he had to say something back, you can say a lot of things about Mr. Tilghman but you can't say he isn't polite. "How are you, Fred?"

"Just fine."

Tig had gotten his hands under control and now he was picking bits off the turkey carcass and stuffing them in his mouth, he wasn't even chewing but he kept picking bits off and stuffing them into his mouth.

"The Space Walk is neat, Mr. Tilghman."

He had to give me the movie star smile, he was half awake and there was the movie star smile. "I'm glad you think so, Fred."

What I hate is the way he always has to pretend everything is fine. I said, "I just wish it worked."

Mr. Tilghman was so polite that he said, "Ralph, why
don't you get it going for Fred here?"

Tig exploded, all spit and turkey bits. "I can't."

Now that I thought about it nobody could, the damn
thing was a piece of junk. Tig had run off and left me
down there in his stupid basement because I was being a
pain in the ass and he knew it wouldn't work, it was
never going to work, and now here was his father trying
to pretend there was nothing the matter with it. Whatever was on my face right then, Tig didn't want to look
at it, he just started picking at the turkey again. So I
had to say, "Gee, Mr. Tilghman, maybe you could help
us get it working."

"Why certainly, Fred."

So he had to go down there in his bathrobe and his
bare feet and fool with it. If Tig had asked him he might
have stomped back up to bed but there I was and he was
stuck, you know, the host. It's hard to explain exactly,
but this is the reason he's always so polite and I guess
it's the reason for all the presents and the manicures and
the way he keeps his face so nice, the thing is, Mr. Tilghman always wants you to think the best of him, and I
guess that's what gives me the creeps.

He was down there which meant we had to stay down
there with him, he was so smooth, he was saying, "Now,
what's the trouble here?"

Tig said, "It's busted."

"Don't be ridiculous. Just plug it in."

"OK, I'll plug it in."

"Well go ahead." Nothing was happening.

Tig said, "I already did."

Pop would have kicked the thing or else started laughing, but not Mr. Tilghman. He had to bend over and start fooling with the wires as if he could really do something, he had to say, "We'll have it going in two seconds."

He didn't

Tig was dying.

So was I.

He kept fooling with it, he would try something and then Tig would have to plug it in again and nothing would happen so Tig would have to unplug it, so he could fool with it some more. I could see Tig was embarrassed and so was I but if either of us suggested maybe we should give up on it Mr. Tilghman would say "Nonsense, we've almost got it," ho ho ho, and we would have to stand there and he would have to keep on fooling with it, it was him and the Space Walk in mortal combat, it was weird.

My legs were tired, Tig looked shaky and we both wanted to be somewhere else, anywhere else, but Mr. Tilghman kept on working, he wouldn't quit so we had to stand there, we might still be there except my mother had phoned me to come home, Mrs. Tilghman called from the top of the basement stairs.

I said, "Mr. Tilghman, I've got to go."

"Not now, I've almost got it working."

"I'm sorry, Mr. Tilghman."

Tig said, "Dad, he has to go."

"But I'm going to have it in another minute."

"I'm sorry, Mr. Tilghman."

"OK, Dad, OK?"

Mr. Tilghman was practically pleading, "If you'd just wait."

Tig wanted me to get out just as I wanted to go, he

was dying to escape too but he threw me a look: *morituri te* or *sauve qui peut* and said, "I'll wait with you, Dad, OK?"

"But I wanted Frederick to see it working." I really think he was going to grab my arm but I was too fast.

I said, "I'll come and see it tomorrow, Mr. Tilghman," and ran away.

I felt sorry for Tig, there we were, we had spent two hours down there with his father that hardly ever had any time for him, maybe Tig was supposed to be thrilled but how could he be? The terrible thing was that what Mr. Tilghman was doing down there didn't have anything to do with me or Tig, it was something he had to get under control because he had said he was going to do it, he said so in front of witnesses. We had to be there to see him doing it, but whatever it was he was really doing, he was doing it for himself.

When I got home our house was dark, I guess Mom had forgotten to turn on any of the lights. She was sitting on the sunporch in front of the TV and she sounded funny when she said hi.

I said, "What's the matter?"

"Nothing."

"You said you wanted me."

"Oh, that. I just haven't seen you all day, that's all. Want to watch TV?"

I wanted her to pat me and tell me everything was cool. "Sure." I plopped on the other end of the sofa and then I saw she was crying, which scared me, I said, "What's the matter?"

"Nothing. Just depressed."

"Did Pop?" If it was something like that, I would know what to do about it, you know, How to Behave. I could protect her and make Pop apologize for whatever it was, but then I thought, whatever it was, Pop wouldn't do it.

"Don't be silly, he didn't do anything."

"Then what's the matter?" I expected her to say, Nothing, even if she didn't mean it.

"I don't know."

So there was just that, the two of us sitting in front of the television, her crying and neither of us knowing why. When the show was over she got up to make supper. I went out and offered to make brownies from a mix, she started to say no because of all the leftover turkey and pies piled up in the refrigerator but then she hugged me and said OK, we shelled the nuts my aunt and uncle sent from Florida and by the time Pop got there the spaghetti was ready and we were more or less OK.

Of course I didn't go back to see the Space Walk like I promised, rather, I went back but not to see the Space Walk because it was broken and nobody ever really expected me to. I went to get Tig so we could pick up Welles at her house and go skating, we never talked about the Space Walk again. After a while we just moved the pieces off the Ping-Pong table and into a corner, and went back to playing Ping-Pong as if it had never happened. I didn't see Mr. Tilghman again until he came to a party at our house, he looked at me like he didn't exactly remember who I was, he would have said, What Space Walk? He had forgotten but I never did.

2.

LAST YEAR we wrote:

> Rantula, *ta ta ta ta ta ta-*
> rantula, *ta ta ta tata ta ta taaaaaa . . .*

and for a while there we were hairy and to be reckoned with because we had something the rest of the world didn't, we were into T. Rantula that Eastern mystic and great transvestite singer, who was in reality your gigantic killer spider, or at least I think he was. It started right after New Year's and from then on we were always bopping off to T. Rantula concerts or writing new end-of-the-world songs with T. himself on the platform in the black satin suit with the black silk leg-fringes, he

would be singing his balls off and mashing entire buildings with, was it the electronic hype, eight thousand
amplifiers wanging, or was it eight great hairy legs?
Right, we made it all up, it was to get at somebody on
our bus.

The worst kids in town get on at our bus stop, the
driver always pulls his earflaps down so he won't have to
look or listen and if we don't lunge for seats he starts
with a jerk that throws everybody in the aisle. That
might be because of Jackie Rasker, who makes gorilla
noises most of the time, or Danny Abel, who can scream
like eight old ladies being raped, or it might be because
Arnie Moon always tries to get the driver to stop so he
can tell on somebody that hit him; when we were in
grammar school Arnie used to cry if you looked like
you were going to hit him but now that we are bigger he
just whines. Maybe the driver only hates our stop because there are so many of us and we are so loud but I
think it's because he has this idea that we are all too
smart for our own good because our parents teach college and use big words that keep slipping into our vocab-
ularies, which is why the other kids hate us, along with
at least half the teachers in our school: *You think your
father knows so much.*

I used to think it would be really neat to have a father
that was a plumber or sold fanbelts or something incon-
spicuous, we could live out there in Park Estates in one
of those neat little split levels along with all the kids
that are on teams and in the student government. I
would be so normal that you wouldn't be able to pick
me out in any crowd, Pop would throw the ball around
with me on weekends and the house would always be
full of hot fruit pies and other people's mothers doing

each other's hair. When I was in the second grade I
played with a kid that came from one of those houses,
his mother was big in the P.T.O. and his father worked
in the airplane factory, when I went over to his house it
was just like being in a commercial, everything looked
new, even his mother, and the place was so little and so
clean. I had him back once but he wouldn't stay. He got
spooked before we got through the front hall because
the place is big and old, we have dark woodwork and
the windows are about eight feet tall, it was so uncom-
mercial that I guess it scared the hell out of him. By the
time we got to my room, he was asking to go home. He
wouldn't come in my room and when I said why not he
said, It looks like a junk pile, your mother didn't even
make your bed, my mother always makes my bed. I
said, So what, she has better things to do, what difference does it make, but he just said, I want to go home. I
thought he was going to cry so I had to beat him up.
Every once in a while I bump into him at school, he
looks stuffed full of vitamins and clean living, I guess he
spends his weekends doing All-American things. Tig and
Welles and I play Star Trek on the college computers on
weekends, and at night we go to movies, they show thir-
ties gangster stuff and forties musicals in the auditorium,
you could get stoned just sitting there because the minute the lights go out half the students light up. Arnie
Moon went out for Little League and Scouts and all that
stuff, he never gave up trying to hang out with the ordinary kids, I think his folks even took Ordinary lessons,
but Tig and Welles and I just gave up pretending, we
were always the ones with the holes in our knees and
the exploding sneakers and the ring around the collar,
we were the ones with the paperback *I Ching* and the

peanut butter sandwiches because our mothers never made our lunch, we never hung around with anybody but each other because we had already faced up to it, Ollie Ordinary we were not.

So there we were, all the worst kids, getting on the bus: me, Welles, Tig, Moon, plus Abel and Rasker, Patty Westover and Farter Fisk, everybody more or less un-ironed and unmended except for Patty, who does her own, and Arnie Moon, whose mother is a housewife by trade, there we were all getting on and mingling with the kids from town: Tuffy Tucci that always tries to kill me, plus his mean brother, and the Korskis and Fern Zumwalt and Ida Cade and the McWhirter twins along with a lot of older, really bad people who got kept back which means they were still in the eighth grade at fif-teen, pushover girls spilling out of T-shirts and big guys with bad breath who hated us because we never studied and always got everything right.

Tig and I got a seat together but Welles was stuck across the aisle with big old Fern Zumwalt, her father runs some kind of company so she has all the clothes she wants, I used to keep notes in French class, waiting for her to wear the same thing twice. Since they were stuck in the same seat Fern started putting it to Welles because something bla bla something, she never showed school spirit or hung out with the rest of the girls; Tig and I were on about this corny old fifties movie they had at the auditorium over New Year's, we weren't pay-ing much attention to what Fern was saying, exactly, but we could catch the tune, and it made us get louder and louder until finally even Fern couldn't hear what she was saying and she leaned across the aisle and yelled, "What Rantula?"

Then Tig grinned and said, "T. Rantula," just like that.
"T. who?"

Welles was saying, "Big as an apartment building."

Corny old movie, with Leo G. Carroll, I said,
"Acromegalia."

Tig said, "Black hair all over the legs."

Tuffy Tucci was sitting in back of us and he hit Tig on
the head with his fist. "Who has black hair all over his
legs?"

Tig said, "T."

I said, "Rantula."

Welles was already making up the tune: *"Rantula, ta
ta ta ta ta ta-rantula . . ."*

Tig said, "You've never heard of T. Rantula?"

So there it was.

Fern Zumwalt always has to know everything, she
couldn't stand it so she said, "Of course I've heard of
T. Rantula, I've got one of his records."

"You mean, you've never been to a concert?"

She minched up her mouth. "No, I've never been to a
concert, and I bet you haven't either."

Welles said, "Well what if I haven't?"

Fern Zumwalt figured she was on top again. "I've even
got his autograph."

Welles said, "I suppose you got it on your underpants."

"Yes I've got his autograph on my underpants."

"Let's see."

"I'm not wearing them, and besides, I've got his picture too."

Tig was breaking up. "Black hair all over the legs."

"He signed me on the stomach." By this time Welles's
eyes were just little old slits. "He was teaching us to
meditate."

"Who?"

"Futch and Tig and me."

Tuffy said, "Bullshit."

Tig was noodling, *"Beat his brains out shove him in the toilet."*

Tuffy pounded Tig on the head again, "I said, bullshit."

Tig just kept on, the tune was beautiful, *"Cause his mother made it with a mangy pig . . ."*

"You better watch out, kid."

"Give him poison now but please don't spoil it."

Tuffy had his mouth open, he couldn't quite figure it out.

Old Welles was smiling, butter wouldn't melt. "You mean you haven't heard that?"

"Heard what?"

We were in front of school now and Tig wound up, *"I want to kill him when I'm big."*

I said, "Hey wow."

Welles said, "Don't ya dig it?"

There was Tuffy with his mouth open, so Welles got up and just before the doors opened she pounded him on the head with her fist for a change: "Man, that's T. Rantula's big hit song."

Then we got out of the bus in a hurry and ran into school.

In French we had Miss Frascati, she was pushing her lips out at us again, trying to get us all to make the "le" sound, there was a greasy line across her stomach where she must have leaned against the sink that morning and I could hear Tig behind me, singing:

> Terrible old lady, says please call her Miz
> Sleeps with all the lights on cause she
>   don't know what love is,

it was another T. Rantula number, I picked up the
styling and when I got benched in gym for the black
socks I noodled a little myself:

*"Kill Coach Short and eat him, mash him where he
stands,"* I could hear the electric guitars coming up
underneath, the amplifiers were tuned up so high that
all you could hear was feedback and the stage lights
would be blinding, like a nova, there was old T. Rantula
up there in the fox fur midriff jacket and the satin pants
with the long black fringe, they would be acting out the
torture and death of Coach Short up there on the platform behind him while T. soul-kissed the microphone,
and everything he sang about the torture, they would
do. Then in Art, which the three of us take sixth period,
Mrs. Lucibella tore up Welles's tree and made her do it
over so it would look like everybody else's because
everybody knew you couldn't be an artist unless you
learned to follow directions, that was the most important thing. I couldn't hear Welles, I could only see her
lips moving but I saw Mrs. Lucibella jump, you would
think she had been goosed, she said, "What was that,
Eleanor?" but Welles looked blank and said, "Nothing,
Mrs Lucibella, just a song."

We even hummed a few bars in Mrs. Galitto's class, I
like her but she is always on my back about the good
old school paper, why am I not on it, well that's for kids
who don't have anything better to do. I hate people
who try to make you better than you are, I mean, who
needs it? By the time we were sprung at two-thirty we
had done everybody who needed doing, if they never
heard any of it that served them right.

We had the good sense to let it drop when we got on
the bus because Tuffy Tucci is dumb but he isn't that
dumb, if he found out we were putting him on he would
beat the shit out of one or all of us. Fern Zumwalt was

at movement class, she would be sweeping around the
Leakey dance studio in her dirty pink leotard, so we
didn't have her on our back with her T. Rantula autograph, that we would have to say, "All right, you're so
damn smart, let's see it," which she wouldn't be able to
do, the tarantula would be out of the bag and that
would be the end of it. For whatever reasons we didn't
want to use it up right away, we were on to something.
All one of us had to do was go, *ta ta ta,* the first three
notes, and we would all three break up laughing.

We got off the bus, going: *ta ta ta,* fooling around on
the corner and laughing until Welles's little sister came
down and said her mother wanted her.

So I had to go home.

Mom was there, like always, looking like somebody
who has been waiting around too long. It was the time
of day when she always began to tip. I never knew exactly how I would find her. She always had stuff to do
in the mornings, she would clean and then she might
paint, after lunch she could go to Mrs. Tilghman's and
have tea but she could only string it out for so long.
Some time in the middle of the afternoon she would run
out of things to do and all her clocks would slow down,
dumping her into an empty place where nothing worked
and nothing was worth doing.

She said: When I die, it will be around this time in the
afternoon.

She was plastered against the window, I thought she
might be crying. I said, "Mom?"

She said, without looking at me, "What do you want?"

"What's the matter?"

When she turned her face was long and white: empty.
"Nothing."

I didn't think that was exactly true. She was still looking at me, more or less waiting for me to leave so she could go back to crying, but I got the idea that I'd better wait long enough to find out what was the matter and apologize or do whatever it took to make things better. "Look, Mom, if it's anything I did or anything. . . ."

"You didn't do anything, Fred. Everything's fine." Her voice was wavering the way it does when she is trying to be calm. "It's, ah, the painting. I should have been a painter."

"You are a painter."

"Just junk. I let it go too late, Fred. It's too late for me."

"Wait a minute."

"Don't let it get too late for you, OK? I could have been a good painter, if your father hadn't . . ."

"Mom, stop it." It hit me in the stomach, thump.

Her voice was light, like a kid's voice. "It was either or."

"Look, Mom, if it's something I did and you want me to . . ."

"This isn't about you."

"Then why are you mad?" I guess I must have sounded scared.

"I'm not mad, I . . ." She turned around and this time she saw me. "Look, you go and play, OK?" Her voice was shaky and she was pretend smiling.

"I thought I would stay and help with dinner. What are we having?" I couldn't just leave her, I had to get her started on the next thing.

She pulled hard against the pull of the window. "Meat loaf, I think."

"Is that all?"

"What do you mean, is that all?" She looked hard at me because she had figured out what I was doing. "OK, jerk, I'll make a pie."

"Apple?"

"Apple." She let me see she was heading for the kitchen. "I promise. Now get out."

So it was all right for me to take off, because she had enough stuff to do to get her through the afternoon. In the kitchen she could turn all the lights on and pretend it was almost time for supper and she was doing something important; as long as she was cooking she would be OK. I didn't want to look around at the house because I was scared she would be back at the window, it would be all rainy on the inside of the glass: her tears running down. When I cried she knew how to make me feel better, but if she cried what was I supposed to do?

It turned out Tig's mother had a headache, which meant Tig was supposed to clear out until suppertime, and Welles's mother was having her French One students at the house, for a minute I thought maybe I could drag them back to our place to cheer up my mother, but what we did was, we played at Farter Fisk's.

Farter is round and funny-looking, he makes this farting sound every time he giggles, and we have never been able to figure out whether he farts and then giggles about it, or whether when he giggles it makes him fart. He has always been one of those people you don't know whether to like or feel sorry for; when he is laughing he is OK but there are other times when he gives off this grey cloud, like strontium 90 or one of those diseases you can catch, and you have to be careful not to get exposed because you might start farting and then people would have to feel sorry for you.

Farter was the first kid whose parents got divorced, or maybe the first one that it happened and we all noticed it. There was this corny old pop song, about when they break the news? It went, "You better sit down, kids," twanga twanga, "and listen to meeee . . ." and every time I saw Farter it would start running through my head. Before it happened he was just like everybody else and then he began showing signs of the dread disease, he started getting fat and his clothes got filthier and filthier and his nose ran all the time. We were in the fourth grade and we would overhear a lot of bad stuff about Farter's mother dragging the three kids off to Minnesota and Farter's father going and dragging them back, there was one crazy night when my father had to go out and help because Mrs. Fisk was hiding in the bushes outside of Farter's house, she had a boyfriend with her and they were waiting for Mr. Fisk to go off to class so they could grab the kids. When Farter wasn't around what we used to play was, Mrs. Fisk hitting Mr. Fisk with a rolling pin, and Mrs. Fisk going off to Reno, what we knew about; when Farter was around we had to keep sneaking looks at him to see if he was crying. By the fifth grade we forgot all about it. Then Welles's little sister Tishy said the fairy princess had come to stay at Farter's house, it turned out Tishy had gone looking for Emily Fisk and this beautiful lady answered the door, when Tishy said, Who are you, she said why she was the fairy princess and she had come to take care of the house and make everything nice for Mr. Fisk.

We played up in Farter's attic, which was insulated years ago for some professor who went up there to try and write his book. Farter had curtains rigged up at one end, sometimes that end is his secret hideout and other times it is a stage, he was tickled to death to have us, he

kept dragging pillows over to the wrestling mat and saying, "What do you want to do?" and we would say, "I
don't know, what do you want to do?"

We were all drinking banana milkshakes that Farter
had made in the blender, that kitchen would make a
plumber puke but Farter found some Styrofoam cups
that were OK and we were all lounging around on the
wrestling mat drinking the shakes and feeling good, it
was one of those days when you forgot about feeling
sorry for Farter, he had it all together and we were
doing something really nice.

I guess Tig felt it too, he said, "Listen, do you want
to join the T. Rantula fan club?"

I thought: *Wait a minute*, but it was OK, he wanted
to give Farter a present.

"What are you talking about?"

Welles said, "T. Rantula."

I said, "You know, that great transvestite singer and
telepath."

Tig said, "It's really more Scientology."

Welles said, "I thought it was meditation."

"I thought it was all three."

Farter said, "I don't get it."

"Neither does Fern Zumwalt." Another day I would
have done a number: you mean you don't know the
great T. Rantula? I said, "We made him up."

"Oh wow." Farter started giggling and farting, or farting and giggling.

"Rantula." We did the whole number, ending, *"Ta ta
ta tata ta taaaa . . ."*

Farter was giggling and farting.

I said, "You ought to see him in the black satin suit
with the leg fringe. Man, he makes a crowd."

"When he goes out," Tig said, "he takes tarantulas as big as collie dogs."

Welles was grinning. "If there's anybody on your back you just send for T. Rantula."

Farter was still giggling and farting, farting and giggling.

"He can off your enemies. Tarantulas in the towels."

"Man, he can move buildings."

"Tarantulas in the toilet."

Farter was rolling on the mat, laughing. "He can get the fairy princess, tarantulas in the panty hose."

"But listen, everybody." Tig was zorting milkshake up his straw and then letting it dribble back. "That isn't all he does. Look, he can take you way inside yourself."

"Wait a minute." Welles was swivelling around.

Tig didn't even hear her, or see that she had her hand up, trying to slow him down. "You just sit in there and nothing bad can get you, you just sit in there where nobody can reach."

"Wow," Farter said. "Oh wow."

"But first you've got to learn the song."

So we taught him the song and after that we made up more verses, whenever we wanted to get out of something we would just say we were going over to somebody's house to listen to T. Rantula records, we could cut school and say it was for T. Rantula concerts, so what if nobody saw about it in the papers, they were just dumb. We made up what T. Rantula's house would be like, everything black and lined in fur, and then we made up some of the stuff he did, once he cleared up all the acne in the eighth grade in Waban and another time he went *Zot* and Patty Westover's parents that always hit her ended up back in the fifth grade, they were stuck in their desks and they could never hit her again; by the time we ran out of things the phone was ringing and the fairy princess was hollering from downstairs, one of us was late for supper, whichever one it was their mother was worried sick, so we all made signs that we each thought was the *thuh* T. Rantula sign, none of them were alike, and then we left Farter sitting there in the middle of his attic, wishing we would stay.

Naturally it was Welles's mother that had called, Welles is always bitching because they are so strict but she does it with this, well, snug look: that it's not such a bad thing because she can count on it. We dropped her off first and then we went to Tig's, there were no lights on so we hung around on the walk for a little, it was already dark which is probably why Tig went ahead and said, "I had the weirdest dream." I didn't say anything so he went on. "It was like I came home from a long way off after a long time. I think I was grown up, and when I got off the MBTA the town was empty and our street was empty, when I got to the house it looked empty, nobody there, no furniture, it was my house except all the ceilings were about twice as high and I went in the front door and it was all quiet, there was the stairway in front of me, twice as tall and twice as long, but I had to go up it and the upstairs hall was twice as long with shadows at the end, where you turn to go into the guest room, it looked a million miles away and I was scared but there was something in the dream, I had to go down it, and when I went around the corner there was more hall, by the time I finally got to the door of the guest room everything in me was pounding but there was something in the dream, I knew it was going to be terrible but I still had to go in so I opened the door and the room was empty, no rug, no furniture, there had never been any furniture, it was like we had moved out before the house was ever built, the whole floor was slanting downward and I had to slide down to the closet, it took a long time but I finally got there and I opened the door and it was all dark inside, like one of those black holes in the universe, so I couldn't see at first and then . . ."

"You fell in."

"No, my father."

"Your father?"

"It was my father in the closet, I think there was blood on his mouth and he was crouched in there, I knew he was going to get me, he was just about to spring."

"Wow. Dr. Freud. No. Call T. Rantula." I went on because it made me feel better. "T. could handle it."

"Yeah, right," Tig said. "T. Rantula."

When I got home I could hear Mom and Pop talking in the kitchen, a lot of nice nothing. I could smell the meat loaf cooking and everything was fine.

3.

POP SAID, "When I was little all you had to do was be good. Now good isn't supposed to be important, you have to be happy, and people are paying out thousands of dollars because they all feel guilty and besides, they can't figure out what happy is."

I said, "Nobody knows what good is either."

"Good is hard, is what it is. But when you manage, you've got something."

"What about happy?"

He said, "Happy is what we never get. Quite. At least not all the way."

"Then what's the point?"

"Once you know that, you've got it licked."

"It isn't fair."

"Good isn't so bad." He was grinning. "Getting there is half the fun."

"You're crazy."

"And that as much as anything explains why I am here."

Where we were was, we were in the middle of the lake in snorkel parkas and thermal underwear and gumboots but freezing our tails off anyway, fishing through this hole Pop had hacked in the ice. It's what we do instead of church. Pop gave all that up a long time before I was ever born, and the only time I heard him try to explain was one Easter when my grandmother was giving him hell about it, he just grinned and said, if he couldn't have all the answers, he wasn't going to waste his time with some outfit that only had a few of them, and that had a lot of stuff wrong with it besides, but I guess he never really got shut of it because we still have to get up early every Sunday and go out and do something hard. We run or swim or go ice fishing because everybody needs to stop and think about being part of something bigger, at least that's what Pop says, so I never let him know that I would rather sleep. He always asks Mom and she always says no; he knows she is going to but he says she has to have the chance to decide.

I didn't mind being cold, we had a little stove and Pop brought cocoa, it was quiet and beautiful, just us with a couple of speed skaters way off, ringing the lake while we sat out in the middle. It was one of those Sundays when I almost understood what Pop was up to; the ice was white and the sky was almost white, there were those black pines and that was about it until you began to look closer and saw the difference between the sky at the tree line and the sky overhead and all the differ-

ent colors in the ice, according to how thick it was and
what was underneath, air bubbles or things floating or
something frozen into it. There I was holding my string
and digging the colors, every once in a while one of the
skaters would flash through, no more trouble than a
bird, dark and fast.

Pop said, "As long as you can go someplace and look
over water, it's OK."

I said, "You mean like the river when you were little."

One of the skaters zitzed in close, spraying ice.

"Someplace that takes the eye." Pop peeled a Hershey
bar and gave most of it to me.

I was looking at one of the skaters looking at me sitting there on the ice with my Daddy, eating chocolate,
and I wanted us to be alone.

Pop was saying, "Otherwise you're just another thing
in a cage. You have to see at least one opening."

It wasn't as open as you might think. The other skater
zitzed in from the other direction. "Hey wow," I said.
"Did you see that?"

All Pop said was, "Take it easy, we don't own the
lake."

"All I want is part of it."

"What difference does it make?"

I hated them seeing us. The day had started out empty
and beautiful and now it was getting crowded, the
skaters were going in circles again but the circles were
getting smaller, closing in on us, every once in a while
one of them would zoom in and spray ice, finally I got
mad and threw our bait can. "Knock it off." I missed.

"Easy," Pop said, "there's room for all of us."

"Did you see what he did?"

"It's OK."

"They're wrecking everything."

"Only if you get pissed off."

They were really close now, I could see they were only big kids, and maybe it was the way Pop didn't yell at them or maybe it was me throwing the bait can, whatever it was, they wanted us off the lake. They kept circling and taking turns spraying ice, Pop just went on fishing like it didn't make any difference but I was getting madder and madder, finally I stood up and yelled, loud, so there was no more pretending it didn't bother us, "Bastards, cut it out."

Then the big one slid in so fast the ice trembled and said, "Cut what out?"

"You know."

The other one slid in behind him and said, "Yeah, what?"

So I said, "You know damn well." I was on my feet, I thought Pop was standing behind me, he probably had his fishing knife out by then so I said, "You don't own the lake."

"Blow it out your ear."

"Watch out or my father will . . ."

"We just came out here to warn you." The big one had his knees bent and now he was jiggling up and down so it seemed like the ice was moving. I don't know, maybe it was. "The ice isn't safe."

"Says who?"

"Says us." The other one was going up and down with an ugly look. "You hear that creak?"

"Go to hell."

"Look, man, it isn't safe."

"Clear off or else."

"Or else what?"

I hefted a piece of ice. "Or else."

"You and what army?"

"My father has a knife." I turned around then and
God, he was just sitting there, putting his string through
the hole as if nothing was going on. "Show 'em, Pop."

"Yeah, Pop, show us."

"I'm not kidding, he has a knife."

All he did was reel in the string. "They might be right,
Fred." He pretended to test the ice and the two guys
bent at the knees, up and down, up and down, you
couldn't tell if they were doing it or the ice was doing
it to them; maybe I did hear something creak. Pop was
already putting everything into his tackle bag, so cool
and slow you would think this was exactly the way he
planned it. "Maybe the ice isn't safe."

The guys were sliding a little on their skates, carving
arcs, just to keep everything moving.

"Pop, you can't let them . . ."

"Well," Pop said, "thanks for the warning."

The big one said, "You're welcome, asshole," and
they took off.

I said, "Bastards, dammit, bastards," and threw my
chunk of ice but it was too late. I wanted to hit Pop.
"All you had to do was show them the knife."

"That would be dumb. What would be the point?"

"Well at least you would have showed them."

"That would make me just as bad as them." Pop had
everything packed up and he had started slogging back
across the ice, but he turned around to look at me.
"There has to be a difference between us and them,
that's the whole thing."

"If that's what good is, I don't want any."

Pop said, "It's a big lake and you're stuck in the middle of it. Don't make waves."

I thought I would take happy and it would serve him right.

Then I watched them working on happy. It was terrible.

They were getting ready for the costume ball. I think they were doing it for Mom. They spent days on it, him painting bumblebee stripes on his yellow slicker and her making this huge silk thing to strap on her ass so she could go to the costume ball as a flower. I would come in and find her brooding over it, putting in bits of deeper rose and green as if she expected a judgment at the end of the big night and if she skipped a stitch or left something out a thunderbolt would fall and leave her naked except for the scarlet letter: F. Everything had to be perfect, they even had their pre-party fight in time for her to get her face cleaned up and patted smooth, the candles were all lit and they were the perfect picture of something when I left.

I was eating at Welles's house along with Tig, they had Mrs. Brill in for Welles's little brother and sister, and she was supposed to keep track of us. We had begun to hear a lot about our responsibilities as young adults but when it came right down to it they were all scared to death we would do—what? We had spaghetti, Mrs. Welles was stomping around the kitchen in a peasant dress and Russian boots, waving a spatula for no reason and making us eat, we could hardly wait for her to put on the wig with the yellow wool braids and clear out, which she did after she served up the Yodels. By that time she had rouge circles on both cheeks and a mouth like a painted wooden doll but you would have known her anywhere because she never really changes, no matter what.

"You kids can make popcorn, and whatever you do, be nice to Mrs. Brill."

We all said we would, even though she is a smelly old lady with yellow-white hair that nobody likes because she is always the one that stays when your mother goes to the hospital or somebody dies or your parents are down talking to their lawyers; she was out in the front room with the little kids and all we had to do to keep her happy was give her lots of popcorn and then stay out of her way. The minute the door closed the kitchen ceiling shot up; the windows and doorframes seemed about ten feet tall and the hanging glass shade made a well of light with us sitting at the bottom of it.

Welles said, "They're gone."

"We can do anything we want."

"Almost." Welles shot her eyes toward the door to the dining room: Mrs. Brill.

I was thinking about my mother spraying perfume on her silk rosebud, the Tilghmans in their rented pirate suits. "What if we went?"

Tig said, "What as?"

"Don't be stupid. We would go as somebody else."

We kicked that around for a while, we would all go in drag with Tig and me in Welles's mother's party dresses and Welles in one of her father's suits, or else we would go as T. Rantula and his rock group, we would bop out on the bandstand and sing the Armageddon number, or else we could sew together a bunch of blankets and slide in as a sea serpent, we could . . .

Welles said, "It wouldn't work."

"Why not?"

"They'd know it was kids."

Tig said, "They'd know it was us."

"Then they would throw us out."

"I guess you're right." I was sliding in my chair by that time, thinking about the party, what they all said when we weren't around. "I bet they're all drunk by now."

Welles said, "Drunk and dancing on the tables. I don't think."

"Just like Mardi Gras." Tig had a wild look. "What if we go see?"

"We can't, they'd kill us."

Tig said, "Not if they don't see us."

"You mean sneak?" Welles was shushing us and pointing toward the other room. "Mrs. Brill."

But Tig and I were already picking up our boots from the newspaper where they had been dripping, reaching for our coats. I said, trying to sound normal, "Just keep talking normally."

Tig said, "If we just keep talking normally she'll never know."

"Look you guys, my parents are going to kill us."

"Are you coming or not?"

"All right," Welles said, " all *right*."

So we just kept talking normally while we got all our stuff on, MLA convention, bla bla bla, full professor, bla bla bla, publish or perish, let me freshen your drink, while we got into our boots, gloves, mufflers, hats, it was just like the sextet from *Lucia* minus three, we kept it up until we got the back door open, by the time Mrs. Brill heard it slam we would be over the hedge and half-way down the block.

Welles runs like an aardvark with her shoulders
hunched and her nose leading; Tig was The Shadow,
hardly even there, and I was absolutely soundless, picking up tarantula legs and laying them down one at a
time, I was taller than the science building, big as the
Big Pru, with my eight black legs arcing over sleeping
villages, not even connecting with the ground, so that
we all ended up in the bushes outside my house without
any of the people inside knowing it.

It was so boring that we left after five minutes. There
were about a dozen people having drinks, killing time
until they could go to the big party and put on the dog.
Mom had already figured out that she couldn't sit down
as long as she was wearing that flower and she was going
around to stand at people's elbows like the silent butler,
the person with the food that nobody really notices, she
would smile and they would take things off the tray and
stuff them in their mouths without ever looking at her, I
guess that's the story of her life. Pop had taken off the
painted slicker and Mr. Welles had his coat over a chair
so none of them really looked much different; they
could have been just anybody on any old day except for
Mr. Tilghman, he has that face that is more like a mask
than a real face anyway, so he looked more like a person
later on at the dance, when he put on the rubber pirate
face.

Tig said, "What a bomb."

They had worked so hard. "Maybe it's better than it
looks."

Welles was being nice, she said, "Maybe you have to
be there."

Tig said, "Is that what we're waiting to grow up for?"

Then she undercut it, rat. "I suppose that's those
dumb shrimps on the soggy bread."

"That was hot crabmeat, smartass." Those were my parents Welles was dumping on. All that work.

Tig was hanging on the windowsill. "If that's all there is, I don't want it." He dropped, *thock,* into the dirt.

We left. None of the other parties looked any better. The provost was having the administration party, nobody was in costume at all and it looked like a meeting of the board, they hadn't even changed their faces for the party so everybody looked alike. Everybody looked alike at Farter's too, except over there it was all beards and stringy hair, the swingers; you would think, yeah, well, except all of Farter's father's friends are *old,* they just had to have that last toke before they went to the ball. We went on over to the boathouse, which was where the dance was going to be but there wasn't anybody there except the orchestra and a table of divorced ladies, Danny Abel's mother and some others, one of them had on black longies and a bunch of gauze tied around her waist, I don't know what she was trying to be but Welles said, I bet she falls down before this whole thing is over, I don't know how she knew. By that time we were cold so we put together all our nickels and dimes and went over to the machines in the freshman lounge, it was still the winter break so there was only one other person in there, some student that couldn't afford to go home to Java or wherever, and he was asleep.

Things looked better at the boathouse when we went back later; more or less everybody was at the party by that time, and we went all the way around the porch looking into all the windows, we finally settled down at one at the far end. The lady in the gauze thing was dancing all by herself by that time, my parents were slow-dancing in a corner, I kept wishing they would look happier about it since they'd worked so hard but he'd left the slicker somewhere and the big flower on her ass was drooping, I guess she had gotten tired of perching on the edge of things and decided it didn't matter if she sat down. Mr. Tilghman was out in the middle, whirling some lady in a ballgown, he is a great big showy dancer except he is always hurting somebody, one of the people in clown suits was already holding his ear where Mr. Tilghman had banged into it and the coach and his wife were scowling out from under their hockey helmets because he had stepped on both of them without noticing, he was halfway across the floor dancing wide in the pirate boots and swinging his arms so people could see his chest and stomach muscles because he wasn't wearing a shirt, just a leather vest. Mrs. Tilghman was taking up the other half of the floor with the new guy in Speech who has a big dog and a little car, he was wearing one of those no-costume costumes, his academic gown and a big straw hat. Arnie Moon's dear old parents were doing some dear little dance over to one side, out of the Tilghmans' reach, he had his hair slicked back like somebody out of a movie and that big square face on, and she had the little brown curls and the Girl Scout cookie smile, I don't know why you always end up hating people that there's nothing wrong with, maybe it's for spending so much time trying to do everything right, and if they would just lose their tempers or be less boring you wouldn't mind them so much.

The people I felt sorriest for were the ones in giant cereal boxes that they must have worked on all year; all they could do was stand there looking terrific, because they couldn't bend and they couldn't eat or drink anything, they could hardly even see out. There were a lot of gypsies, people who couldn't figure out costumes and just put on bracelets and handkerchiefs with what they wear every day and then there was a whole bunch that we couldn't figure out because they weren't really trying to be anything in particular but they had put on all the makeup and wigs and extra clothes and masks they could find—anything to make them look like somebody else. Since nobody was supposed to know who they really were that meant they could act like somebody else which was what they were all doing, they were all clumped up in corners rubbing and hugging people that didn't belong to them, I guess they were having a good time but if they had to go back to being themselves the next day, what was the point?

After a while they had the costume parade, and the lady in the black underwear and all the gauze came out and twirled with her hands on her head, the coach and his wife were chuffing around in the hockey helmets and I could see my mother pulling herself up because she still believed in the rose she had made, maybe she even thought they were going to win because Pop had found his slicker and put on the beanie with the antennae, they didn't look half bad, but of course the prize went to the cereal boxes because they deserved it.

So there was that, and then everybody went back to dancing, people were beginning to get drunk by that time, the ones that were trying so hard to be somebody else were grinding and snuggling and licking and the lady with the gauze was still whirling in one place but by that time her false eyelashes were half off and her mouth was smeared, and Mr. Tilghman was dancing with some lady in a homemade leopard suit that showed a lot of everything except her face, he had just stepped on poor old

Miss Dowdy and she was holding her shin where the blood had started seeping. Mr. Fisk's gang were all bunched up dancing together and the Welleses were dancing around the edges, laughing and talking like they were having a good time, but the ones that were having the best time were the old parties in their white jackets that had turned yellow and their wives in the shiny dresses that had gotten too big for them, along with leftover old ladies in velvet dresses, they were all at one table, just taking in the show. It doesn't matter what's going on at the college or how boring it is, they will all go to it, they sit up front with big smiles and whatever it is they just love it, I don't know if they're just brave, or happy that they don't have to try any more, or maybe they just don't expect as much, I thought it was all right for them but I wanted more.

Tig said, "If this is all, I'm going home."

"Wait."

A fat guy brought his wife over by our window so they could have a fight. She had on a Carmen Miranda hat like the one we saw in *The Gang's All Here* and she shook her head so the fruit wobbled.

Tig grabbed my arm. "Watch out, they're going to see you."

"Shut up, I'm trying to hear." I sat down because he made me. "Nothing is happening, *nothing*."

Tig said, "They should let us have the party, they could stay home with Mrs. Brill."

"They don't know how to do *anything*."

Welles turned on me. "What did you expect?"

"I'd really like to show them, make them pay attention."

Welles said, "I don't know what you mean."

Tig said, "You mean so they would have more fun."

"No, so they could see how they look."

"You don't know how you look." Welles was always trying to be fair. "I mean not really."

"I have a pretty good idea." I did, too. We were the kids huddling outside the window, or the peasants watching them dance right before the revolution, except the peasants were watching a blaze of light and glamour, something that made it worth starving out there in the snow. "This stinks."

Tig got up. "Let's leave."

"Maybe we got a bad window."

Welles was shuffling. "Let's go back to my house."

"No, around the other side." I was up, but I wasn't leaving.

"You're crazy."

"We just got the wrong window. There's going to be more."

"What difference does it make?" Welles was flapping her arms and dancing in place; she knew she couldn't get Tig to leave unless I left too. "I'm cold."

"I'm staying." What was I waiting to see?

"Me too."

"Hey, you guys . . ."

"All right, Welles, are you coming or not?"

"All right, all *right*."

We were keeping low, so they wouldn't look out the windows and catch us, and the first thing was that there were kids up at the corner window, we all did panto-mimes about keeping quiet and kept on going.

We went around the corner with our heads down and bumped into more kids, Rich Oliver was hoving up out of the darkness, that we used to go to school with, I

don't know what he was doing home from boarding
school but there he was ranging around the porch looking for some of the same things we were, we said, "Shut
up," and he said, "Shut *up*," and wheeled on around the
other side to look in our window; I guess we were going
around to look into his. At the front door we bumped
into Patty and some girls she hangs out with, they were
clumped looking through the glass.

Tig tried a campus cop voice. "You girls had better
watch it."

They jumped and then laughed when they saw it was
only us.

When we went around the next corner there was
Farter glued to the first window, looking cold. It was
spooky because we had started out thinking we were all
alone doing something special, that there were just three
of us and we were more or less invisible, and now it
turned out everybody had the same idea, people kept
looming up in the dark, we were all out there thumping
our hands and freezing our asses while the party went
on inside, and I thought: I bet we are having a better
time than they are, at least we are all out here together
because we want to be, half the people at that party
looked like they were dragged in by force. When I looked
down the porch I could see kids at the next window and
here was Arnie Moon looming up out of the night like
the Ghost of Christmas Future, even Arnie had to come
and I don't know what drew us, I think it was wanting
to see what they were like when we were not around,
the parents, and I don't know about anybody else there
but I was, I don't know, depressed; I wanted there to
be more, I wanted it to be better or maybe I wanted
them to be better, handsomer, happier, because they

had already got to where we were heading and they owed it to us. Right, they owed it to us.

At least there were a lot of us, I think it cheered everybody up and we started getting loud, we kept bumping into other kids and giggling, Tig poked Farter and they were laughing out loud, then somebody else goosed Arnie Moon and he squeaked, Rich Oliver zoomed past in the night; pretty soon we were yelling and running up and down the porches, maybe we just wanted to show them how it was done. By that time the porches were rattling but the parents inside were doing their best to ignore it because if they saw who it was they might have to come out and do something about it, but the Pinkertons who were paid to guard the party came out and chased us off.

Tig and Welles and I just circled around back and hid out in the bushes until we were half frozen, then we sneaked in a side door and hid in the coat room, it was almost dark and we made nests behind one of the racks of coats, getting warm. We couldn't see anything from where we were hiding and we would have left except that by that time the first bunch had started coming in to get their coats, it wasn't even midnight but they were saying things like, It's way past my bedtime, and, I hate these things. There was no way for us to get away for the time being so we were there when Patty's mother had the fight with her father because she wanted to leave and he wanted to stay and dance, she told him to go to hell she would leave without him, he threw the keys at her and when he held out her coat so she could slip into it she just stepped away and let it fall on the floor.

Then this man and this lady came in and closed the door and started grabbing and gobbling, I thought they

might be going to Do It right there with us trapped underneath the coats. It was hot, I was hot, I could hear
Tig's breath catching and I was scared to look at Welles
but then the door opened and Professor Bone came tot-
tering in with his ostrich feather dragging, he said something like, I say, and asked if they would help him find
Lavinia's coat. Then they jumped apart, God, it was two
old people, some scientist and this kid I know's *mother,*
they found the coat and got rid of him but it was too
late for them because two guys came in dragging the
gauze lady that had passed out. Everybody was trying
to leave at once when this student came in, he said he
had to see Mr. Tilghman, uh, uh, uh, would somebody
ask him to come in. The guys with the gauze lady got
a coat around her but this student wouldn't let them go
until they promised to send Mr. Tilghman in and then
he stood there waiting, going uh, uh, uh.

We listened to him bumping around the coat room, I
thought he was going to fall into the coats and discover
us. He was either sighing or wheezing and I thought boy
when I get to college, I am never going to go sucking
around.

Mr. Tilghman was mad as hell. "What are you doing
here?"

"You have to promise."

I would be mad too, being dragged out of a party. He
said, "Promise what?"

"To forget." I guess the stupid bastard had come to
whine about a D, or an F. Pop says some of them will
do anything to bring up a grade and you have to treat
them like steel.

"This is no place to talk about it." I didn't have to see
Mr. Tilghman to know what he looked like: stone.

"I had to, I had . . ."

There was this spitty sound next to me: Tig gnawing on the skin around his fingernails, when he is really bad he chews until there is blood; his big old father would never do that, I guess he really hates him. His big old father was turning around in his pirate boots, he wasn't giving an inch and for once I was on his side.

"You may see me in my office Monday."

"Wait, please."

"Monday." He left.

"God."

What was the big deal? Whatever it was, it was too late, the coat room was filling up so the student gave up; he bumped into about five people on his way out. When the party's over you're supposed to be sad because the party's over, but these people were really depressing; they were all bitching or moping because the party had never begun, even my folks. They were fighting when they came in, Mom's poor silk flower was dragging, by that time the coats had thinned out so I had to see. She was crying and apologizing for it, "I'm sorry, Ted. It *hurts*."

"Nina, I'm trying."

What does she want anyway? The three-ring circus or the yellow pony and the brass band before breakfast? What's the matter with her? "It hurts all the time now."

"Nina." When he tried to reach for her she shook him off.

"All—the—time." It was embarrassing. I wanted to spring at her and shut her up. I wanted to disappear. I wanted them to disappear. Tig and Welles were embarrassed too. They were squatting there pretending to be something else: galoshes, overcoats.

There she was chopping the air and there he was trying to stop her wrists, saying, "Nina, please. Tell me
what to do."

Well she wouldn't answer him.

I don't know what her problem was, that their little
party was a bomb, that her costume was coming apart,
but she was getting mad and I didn't know what to do
about it—whether to pretend it wasn't happening or
whether I should grab Tig and Welles and charge right
through them, maybe we could get away without them
finding out it was us.

"Nina, if you'd just tell me what to do."

Then she turned around and it sounded like she hit
him. "If I thought you could do anything Ted I'd tell
you what it was and you could do it, all right?"

"I've tried everything I can think of."

She stood there with her silk flower shaking, she was
only ever whispering but it could have been a shout.
"Why don't you try leaving me alone?"

"I love you." God, Pop. Don't let her blame you.

"Oh Ted, go to hell." She was still mad; he was rush-
ing at her with her coat, trying to get it around her so
he could take her home; I wished he had a bag to put
over her head, Midas muffler, anything to shut her up.
She was crying hard, running away from him and the
coat; he and the coat followed her and they were gone.

I was feeling like Benedict Arnold for being there.
Mom and Pop always want to pretend they haven't been
fighting; if nobody saw, it wasn't real, but there we were,
witnesses. I got up, wrestling coat hangers. "Let's go."

Tig said, "It's just getting good."

"I have to go."

"It's all right," Welles said. "That wasn't anything."

Tig said, "Nothing happened."

Welles said, "Besides, I was just getting warm."

I could hardly keep still. "My feet are asleep."

"We can't go now, they'll see us."

Welles said, "There are too many people around."

"I don't care." I pulled on Tig.

Tig wasn't budging. "It's my turn. We got to see yours, now I want to see mine."

"We already *saw* yours."

"Not that," Tig said. "It's not the same." So he planted his ass and Welles didn't care what we did now that she was out of the cold but I was all over needles, my nose ran and even the inside of my mouth itched, I said, "I'm getting out."

"Shut up, somebody's coming."

"If they catch us we'll get hell."

I was twitching, I couldn't stand it. "I don't care."

So what the next people saw was me popping out of the coats like somebody coming out of a birthday cake and I will say one thing for us, we stick together, Tig and Welles popped out after me, we all had our jackets over our heads like crooks hiding from the TV, so nobody would know for sure who it was and before they could figure it out we would be gone.

When we got out we split up; Tig was probably going back to Welles's house to wait for his parents, but I didn't want to see anybody right then, or anybody to see me, so I took off alone. There were a lot of people going up the steps to the parking lot so we scrambled up the bank, grabbing bushes to keep on our feet. At the top Tig and Welles kept on going; they looked back to see if I was coming but I just waved. I had to turn around and look. There was the boathouse with the frozen river behind it and music coming out and lights spilling on all the porches, beautiful, like one of those

places in a painting where everybody is happy and
everything is always fine, except I'd been up close and
it wasn't, it was full of ordinary people not even having
fun. Then I thought about the college and the way it
must look to the people who come, perfect place where
there are only wise people, they probably think you can
come here and find the, ah, the Answers, but I guess it
depends on what you are asking. It's scary to think how
many poets and writers and painters and thinkers pissed
and sweated for how long to think up the stuff they
keep collected here, what the college is saving to pass on
to the ones who come after, and how much more was
lost or thrown away because colleges keep only the best.
There it all is: everything worth keeping, and it's our
parents who take care of it and pass it down. It's all
right, they're good at it, you can trust them because
they take good care and some of them will even add to
the heap of things worth keeping, but when it comes to
a simple little thing like having fun at a party they just
can't manage it, which is what stopped me there at the
top of the bank while Tig and Welles ran back to Welles's
house. Have they done something wrong or do they
know too much or what? If they know all that stuff and
they still can't manage it, can I? If it was something like
smoking that you could just not do, or something you
could do, like taking vitamins, and that would take care
of it, things would be a lot easier, but it isn't anything
you can put your finger on. I don't know whether
things go wrong when you hit a certain age or all the
things they know have crowded out all the things they
used to understand or what; there's got to be something
to explain it, otherwise how could people who know so
much be so bad at life?

4.

AFTER THAT I started staring hard at teachers, wondering what they would look like in costume, whether those were costumes, what they would look like with their clothes off, I wondered whether they were good dancers and what they did in bed and whether they felt good about themselves, did they know how to be happy. You are supposed to do what your folks and your teachers tell you because they are the adults and they are supposed to know all about it, but once you figure out they don't know everything, you start wondering whether they know any of it, which is why I put our principal into the rabbit suit with the drop seat and the face cut out; I wanted to see if he looked right in it, and I wanted the coach to look all wrong in

the Tin Woodman suit with the oil drum body and the
number ten juice cans strangling his arms and legs. I put
Mrs. Galitto into a cheerleader suit with the pink legs
sticking out of three inches of skirt, if she tried once
more to get me on the newspaper I would take it off
and there she would be, pink all over, saying, Ray,
Freddy. You can do it. Rah.

Tig and I were already writing *The Ballad of T.
Rantula,* a longer unfinished epic about the end of the
world; when you're in the act, making something like
that up, everything seems to fit into it—either that or
you won't see anything unless you happen to be in the
act. Whatever it was, everything that happened seemed
to fit into it, I had the principal hopping into hell in his
big white bunny suit, right before they fried him he
turned around and twitched his whiskers and said, why?
I said, I don't know, you're supposed to be the one that
knows. I think there were three of us standing arched
over the destruction, black against the red sky with all
those feet set just *so* in between the places that were
burning, so that none of the fires touched us; we were
tarantulas as big as apartment buildings, and at the same
time we were that same beautiful rock singer in the
black satin costume with the black silk fringe and we
were singing, as long as we kept it up the fires would
burn.

*It was in that time of fire and smoke, a lot of folks
were missing and the rest were all broke, no love no
money not even any hope, but I was swinging along;* Tig
would sing softly and I would come up behind the story
part with, *These are the last days the last days the last,
it's gotta be the end because it's worse than the past,*
and Welles would back us up with, *Rantula, ta ta ta ta ta*

ta-rantula, then I would pick up on the story with, *Lights burned out in every back hall, all the people started tripping and the doctor would call, they would say please help us but he couldn't cope, still I was swinging along;* Tig would be singing underneath: *All we can do now is eat-pain and curse, this must be the end cause it can't get any worse,* with Welles doing the ta-ta part and then jumping in with the next verse because it was her turn.

If I had been around home more maybe I would have seen what was going on with Mom but maybe that's why I wasn't around home more, she would either grab me and hug too hard or else I would come in and say a whole paragraph and she wouldn't even hear. If she was crying I wasn't supposed to ask her why, it only made her feel worse because she didn't know, so there was that: her crying and neither of us knowing why. We spent a lot of time at Welles's house because there are plenty of people coming and going and her mother doesn't mind, and the rest of the time we went to Tig's. His mother was off on a skiing trip to Gstaad or someplace, Mr. Tilghman had classes so he couldn't go. He would be home once or twice a week stirring up some French sauce because there was a student coming to dinner but the rest of the time he was hardly ever there. We tried sitting in their big long living room with the velvet furniture and the fancy drapes and we prowled around the library where Mr. Tilghman had everything just so but mostly we hung out in the basement, we would take down a box of Lucky Charms or Cocoa Puffs and in February we worked our way through all Tig's board games, starting with Risk.

Then Welles got the lead in the eighth grade play in-

stead of Fern Zumwalt, and about that time Tig started
running, he had the idea that if he began right now he
would get on the track team when we went to high
school in September. It didn't do any good to tell him
that was months away, he had decided he had to get in
shape, it started small but it got bigger and after a while
it ate him up but that was later on. At the time it only
cut into the afternoons, when Welles was at rehearsal
and I couldn't plan anything with Tig because he would
be at the track and by the time he got finished it was
too late, if I wanted to tell him anything I had to go
wait by the bleachers, I was supposed to yell at him as
he zoomed past because he couldn't slow down. I tried
running with him a couple of times but I would get tired
after the first lap while he just kept on going, he was
like a machine and I don't know who was driving, it
wasn't always Tig. When I did get to talk to him I didn't
like it. I came home late one day, it was that ugly mid-
winter dark and the campus was more or less empty. I
thought even Tig would be gone but instead I crossed
the athletic field and there he was. He was sitting on the
bottom row of the bleachers having the dry heaves.
When he finished I walked him home, Tig was looking
skinny and, I don't know, transparent in the afternoon
light.

"The mother's back from Gstaad."

"Oh, yeah? What did she bring you?"

"Headset radio from the airport gift shop, so I can listen while I run."

"Neat."

"She picked it up at the last minute. She was going to
bring me a sweater but she forgot."

"How long are you going to keep running?"

"Until I show him."

"Who, the coach?"

"The father," Tig said. "He thinks I can't do anything."

"Tell him to go to hell."

"He'd say See, I knew you couldn't do anything. Damn, bloody."

Damn bloody cardboard Mr. Tilghman. "What difference does it make?"

I didn't want to look into the face he turned to me. All he said was, "You know damn well."

There was still Farter, good old Farter that we always condescended to. Tig was off and running and I could never find Welles because of play practice so I started hanging out with Farter, we would make banana milkshakes in their smelly kitchen and then go upstairs and talk. Farter spent a lot of time alone that he would spook around I guess you would call it spying, he would lay out all these little bits and pieces just like baseball cards: what he thought he knew. It was stuff you didn't really want to look at so usually I would try and get him off on school or kids we knew. The last time I went there we chewed over the play, how we could have been in it if we had bothered to go to tryouts, and then I doubled back on the costume party because Farter didn't seem to have too many things he wanted to talk about.

He said, "What do you mean they don't have fun? You should have stayed until the end."

"I did, sort of."

"No, after that." He was poking his straw into his milkshake and eating what stuck to the end. "Who went home with who. There's a lot more going on around here than you think."

I didn't really want to know; well, I did, but the stuff

I found out I would have been better off not knowing. I said, "I suppose Mr. Tilghman."

"Guess again." Farter looked wise.

"Mrs."

"With that big guy in the Princeton gown and the fright wig."

"Oh wow."

"Mr. Tilghman doesn't care."

"How do you know?"

"Everybody's got to get it somewhere," Farter said. "At least that's what my father says."

Welles said Mrs. Fisk left Farter's father because he was fooling around. I said, "If anybody did that to me I would divorce them."

"That's your hangup," Farter said. "The important thing is, you have to grow up free."

It was getting dark in Farter's attic. "Who says?"

"That's what my father says. He says it's the new age. Besides, it wasn't only Mrs. Tilghman. I followed the Lewises and the Warners, they all went to the Lewises' house and I went up under the windows, if they hadn't pulled the curtains I could tell you a thing or two."

"Oh for Pete's sake, Farter. They were probably having drinks."

"That's what you think. I bet you don't even know where Patty's mother went that time."

"Mom said she had a nervous breakdown."

"Bull. She went off with this sophomore, from the college? He was Patty's father's favorite student, they were working on an article together."

"You mean a *sophomore?*" I didn't know if it was funny or terrible or what.

"He sent the paper back from France. Mr. Westover

gave him an A." Farter was slouching back on his pillows, gulping the last of his milkshake with his eyes
shut. "I bet you don't even know what they did."

"What do you think I am, a baby?" My milkshake was
melting and I didn't want the rest of it.

"You think you know, but do you really?" Farter
reached for my milkshake. "I used to think I knew, but
boy."

All right, he was going to lie; that wouldn't hurt so I
would let him. "I suppose you're going to say you did
it with somebody from school."

"Maybe not, but boy." He was rolling his eyes just
waiting for me to ask.

"All right, Farter, what do you know that I don't
know?"

"Before he got divorced my father was uptight just
like yours, but that's all different now, he says he doesn't
want me to waste my life the way he did, you know,
with a lot of hangups? So first he gave me the book."

"Everybody's parents give them the book."

"Yeah, but then he answered, you know, a lot of
questions?"

"Well so did mine." They hadn't. Pop had said if I had
any questions but he didn't mean it.

"Yeah, but then he said he thought that wasn't
enough, and all right, are you ready?" He could hardly
wait. "You promise not to tell?"

I promised.

"He let me watch them doing it."

"Bullshit."

"He did so, and if you don't believe it you can go to
hell."

"The hell with that, you go to hell."

"See first he takes her clothes off and then . . ."

"I've got to go, Farter."

"Don't you want to know?"

I was getting up. I did want to know and I didn't, partly I was sure he was lying, some kid is always trying to tell you that, and if he was lying and I swallowed it, I would never hear the end of it. Either that or he wasn't lying and he was going to tell me a lot of stuff I didn't want to hear, at least I didn't want to hear it from him. All Farter can think about is which things you can put into which other things, if there is anything more to it, Farter doesn't know. "I already know, stupid. Now I've got to go."

"Have it your way." Farter's voice was going up because he didn't want me to leave him alone. "If you're uptight about it that's your hangup and besides . . ."

I was at the top of the stairs by that time but I turned around. "Besides what?"

"He did it because he wants me to be free."

Well he didn't look free, he just looked like Farter sitting on the mat, a little too pale, a little too fat and gassy but giggling because he was farting and he didn't want me to hear. "That's swell, Farter. See ya."

"All right for you, Futch, if you don't believe me I'll take you down to their room and show you where I sat."

"Sorry, I've got to go." I probably owed him something so I said, "Patty Westover's mother really did it with a sophomore?"

"If you stay I'll tell you what I know about Tig's father."

"Never mind."

"Wait a minute, don't you want to know about Mr. Tilghman?"

"Not really." I started down.

"All right, you want to play Monopoly?"

"Can't."

"Remember the fifth grade, when my mother took the sleeping pills?" He had followed me over to the stairs and now he was hanging over the rail, trying to stop me dead with his glare. I thought he would say almost anything to keep me. "I came home after school and I couldn't wake her up so then I went to the office, to get Daddy?"

I sat on the step.

"I went over there to get him and it was really crazy, I could hardly get him to listen. You want to know what they were doing?" He was giggling, except he had his hand over his mouth so I couldn't be sure which it was. "He and this girl assistant and some student were running up and down the halls with these manila envelopes filled with water, she was the fairy princess but I didn't know it then, they were yelling and laughing so hard they didn't even see me."

"I don't get it."

"That's because you have all those hangups. Filled with water, don't you get it?" He was snickering and farting, farting and snickering. "They were having a water fight." When I didn't say anything he said, "You have to know how to have fun."

"Yeah, well, I've got to go."

"We could go to the movies." He had to call after me because by that time I was headed down the hall to the front stairs. I heard him saying, "My father will pay."

Well Mr. Fisk and the fairy princess were coming in as I came downstairs, him with his big belly hanging over the jeans and her in some kind of smock; it was dim in the front hall and they didn't seem to notice me, they weren't even noticing each other, they just stood there with their arms hanging, tired. I looked hard at them but I just couldn't see them in a water fight, at least not lately; I tried to imagine Farter in the bedroom, watching what they did, no hangups, but I just couldn't see it. Right, we are supposed to be free, nothing is wrong if it feels good, but if that is really true why is Tig dead, and why did my mother run away, and why do Farter's father's shoulders drag and why do his arms hang down like that? I had to get away from them and I ran past and out the front door, I couldn't shake the pictures of the plumbing, I was thinking, what, it's got to be better than ugly, there's got to be more to it than that, I was heading for home and our kitchen, I was thinking, maybe Mom.

The house was dark downstairs. She had the lights on in the back room and she was standing there with her paints out; I came in with God knows what on my face; whatever it was, she didn't even see.

"Mom."

"I'll never get it right."

"What?" I don't know what I thought I would get from her: there there, from when I was little. The big smile. Even if she was lying I wanted her to stop and look straight at me and tell me everything was going to be all right.

Instead she turned back to the canvas. "It's such a waste," she said.

"It looks OK to me." It didn't. It looked horrible. I don't even know if that was what she was talking about. "It looks fine."

"A terrible terrible waste of time."

Farter's milkshake was repeating on me, I thought I

was getting a headache, I was sorry I had ever walked in there. "Mom, is there something the matter?"

"What? Huh?" So she finally looked at me. I don't know what she saw but she turned her back on the painting and said "Of course not." She came over and hugged me. "Fred, it's all right. Let's go down and start dinner, OK?" Right before she let me go she said the strangest thing, at least I think she did: "No matter what happens, it isn't you."

There was T. Rantula at the back of my mind, twanga twanga; *These are the new days the new yes the new, what in the hell am I gonna do,* I ran away from it, downstairs to help her get supper. By the time I got through helping her decide what to have it was OK. Mom cut things up and I set the table; I don't know why exactly but we both had to go through all the right motions, she had on the kitchen radio so we wouldn't have to talk, when Pop came in he would read his paper at the kitchen table and for the time being we could be just exactly what we looked like: the American family getting ready for dinner. All right, when Pop and I talked about it afterward he said what the three of us were doing for a long time there was going through the motions, but when things aren't so good maybe that's what keeps people's heads together: going through the motions. Tig was still running and Welles was rehearsing around the clock by that time so I didn't know whether I would ever get her back, so I did the other thing, the heavy school trip, doing the paper, hanging around after it was finished, and if that was going through the motions then maybe there are times when there's nothing the matter with that. If things are heavy there is always junior high: oh wow, glee club; hot dog, eighth grade

dance; the classes meet on schedule and the bells all ring
on time and I can think of worse things than knowing
where you are going to be at three o'clock on Thurs-
days, bashing out the school paper on those junky type-
writers in the mimeograph room.

In Social Studies Mrs. Estabrook was telling about her
childhood in North Carolina, they were so poor that all
they ate was biscuits and drippings. One night somebody gave them pork chops, there was one extra and
Mrs. Estabrook got so excited that she grabbed it off the
plate before she had even finished her first one and ran
into the woods. She wasn't as fat as she is now so she
made it out the door before they even noticed, by the
time the whole family spilled out hooting and hollering
she was halfway up the hill behind a bush, she stayed up
there half the night waiting for them to quit looking
for her. When they finally gave up and went back inside
she was freezing and her pork chop was cold as a bone
and coated with grease. One of the kids asked her how
it tasted, I guess we thought she was going to say it
tasted terrible, you know, because of the guilt, but Mrs.
Estabrook just ran her hands over her belly and said,
"It tasted wonderful, it was the best thing I ever ate." I
guess I thought if I hung around long enough she would
put me in the play after all but they all knew it by heart
by that time so I guess she didn't even think of it.

What she did do was let me into a couple of rehearsals,
it was dark in the auditorium except for the lights onstage and it was better than being at the movies because
I was, I don't know, safe in the dark just watching it
happen, while the good Tucci blew his lines and the bad
Tucci prompted and Mrs. Estabrook yelled at both of
them; it's hard to explain but when you don't know

what you can count on it's good to know there's something you can always count on: good old algebra test, good old school paper, good old eighth grade play.

In March Danny Abel and one of the Zileskis stole some chemicals from the science lab and mixed them with some stuff in Danny's basement. They divided it in test tubes and Ziggy Zileski was halfway home with his when it blew up. The Zileskis are going to go to Florida for good when they finish suing Mrs. Abel's insurance company for what happened to the left side of Ziggy's butt, he had the test tube in his back pocket at the time. Danny said it served him right for being a dork, he was about to steal it so Danny said OK take it, it's no skin off my ass. He went to visit Ziggy at his house after he got out of the hospital and he said it was jammed with that furniture they advertise in the funnies, they even had a color picture of John F. Kennedy that lit up from behind, and Mrs. Zileski was so polite and everything was so clean that Danny felt terrible, not about blowing Ziggy up but because she had even made cookies for him: look here, massa honey, we're not mad. Some kid set a fire behind the biology building and Farter and Jackie Rasker followed Arnie Moon for three weeks until he confessed just to get them to stop sitting on his chest. Patty Westover ran away to Providence, hitch-hiking, it took five days to find her; Tig was still running and my folks were swallowing sentences every time I walked into the room.

Yeah something was up, one night Mom and Pop got all dressed up and took me out to dinner, I don't know what they had in mind but their smiles went bad and they kept clearing their throats. I just hadn't bothered because I would rather eat beans out of the can than sit in an expensive restaurant with two people who have run out of things to say. All they could think of was, Well, or Mmm, more steak? Pop looked at me and said, Well Fred, what do you think of the energy crisis, they had forgotten how to talk to each other and they couldn't even talk to me. The food was drying up in our mouths so after a while we just finished chewing and went to the movies so nobody would have to talk. Mom had her mind on something else all the time then, Pop was mostly at the office and we weren't even doing the Sunday morning thing. When he finally did get up he would shuck me in the car and take me to his office, he said he had to work on his manuscript. What he has is about ten pages with a lot of red markings, except by the time the month was over there were blue markings beside the red markings and he was beginning to put green markings in with the other markings so it looked like a diagram of the central nervous system instead of what it was supposed to be: his book. He would sit there and sigh and rattle papers and I would read until it was time to go home for lunch. I guess Mom was trying to tell us something because the food was terrible, the meat was dry and the dessert was runny, maybe she had cried into it; even the lima beans were like snot. It was a funny winter. Maybe it was partly the weather, that we were still bundled up, puffy coats, hats, too many sweaters, but we all seemed to be in cocoons: Mom, Pop, Tig and I, all bundling along together without ever really touching, getting weird. We didn't come out until the play.

I think I told myself I was mad at Welles by that time, she was spending all her damn time in the auditorium or at home doing homework and the only time we ever talked any more was on the bus. She tried to get me to take some gum that morning and when I said I didn't want any she said, "All right, be that way. I bet you aren't even coming to the play."

Maybe I had thought I wouldn't but with her challenging me like that I had to say, "The hell you say."

Then she looked so pleased I had to say "Damn right I'm coming. So's Tig."

"He never."

"I'll make him."

And I did.

I said, at lunch, "You've got to do it, it's Welles."

He said, "I've got to run."

I said, "You can run tomorrow."

"You don't know anything."

I wanted to hit him but I didn't. "You can't run anyway, it's raining."

"All right," he said, "I'll run afterward, in the gym."

So there we were in the auditorium and it was that thing of being safe in the dark again but this was the big opening and everybody was in costume and full makeup, the good Tucci and the bad Tucci transformed into Vandergelder's clerks, it was *The Matchmaker,* and there was Welles that we had played with for about a hundred years in a gown that pulled in her waist and made even her look worth undressing, stop it, she looked about thirty years old in all that makeup and even her voice was changed, she didn't sound so much like Welles as she sounded like some woman that you would want to know when you were older, beautiful, and when they brought up the flowers after the curtain calls she did a sort of curtsey so she could take them and I thought, oh shit, because there was no way she could ever be the

same person after this, and there was Tig sitting next to
me the way he had a million other times except he was
changing, fixed on whatever it was he was running after
that would never let him rest. Even sitting there in the
audience watching Welles take the roses he was jiggling,
I could feel the whole row vibrating because Tig was
jouncing his knees. *These are the last days the last yes
the last;* there we were working our way out of the
auditorium and it was spinning itself out in my head,
thin but clear, *The Ballad of T. Rantula,* but even if I
sang it out loud Tig wasn't going to pick up on it and if
I managed to do two parts in my head more or less at
the same time there was no way I could bring in the
backup, *rantula,* no way.

I dragged Tig out in the hall after, while they were
taking the cast pictures, and I made him promise to
come backstage with me to see if we could pick up
Welles. By the time they let us back in the hall it was
getting late and there was a cast party going on on stage,
there were so many kids running around that for a minute I couldn't find her. Then I saw her at last, she was
back in her jeans and she was tearing at her hair with her
fingers, trying to get rid of the Shirley Temple curls. She
wiped off the lipstick on her sweatshirt sleeve and when
the bad Tucci thwacked her on the shoulder she gave
him the finger, looking almost crosseyed at Tig and me:
It's OK, see? She meant: *It's me.* I heard Tig say, "Gotta
go while the gym's still open" so he got away from me.

There I was standing by myself, I guess I would have
pulled up my face and gone home but Welles was saying
something to Mrs. Estabrook and Mrs. Estabrook came
over and asked me to stay: Honey you have to or they'll
think you didn't like the play. I looked at her and at

Welles and all those kids dancing and spilling Coke backstage and I thought I would rather be part of that than
anything, so I thanked her and went down the hall to
call home and tell them I would be late.

Pop answered, and he wouldn't even listen. "Here," he
said. "I want you here."

"Pop, it's a *party*."

"I don't care if it's the Queen of France. Get moving."

They were both in the front room waiting for me,
along with a pile of junk that didn't make any sense:
the old easel and a Coop bookbag, one of Mom's suit-
cases from college with the old initials, my backpack
with panty hose dragging from the flap. Mom looked
different, she had been crying and she was dressed to go
out, not one of the pretty outfits with the matching
sweater but the kind of stuff you put on when it's zero
out and somebody has just yelled FIRE. I thought they
were going to apologize for dragging me out of the first
party I had been invited to all year but Pop just looked
at his hands like they didn't belong to him and wouldn't
talk to me. It was good old Mom who came over and
pulled me into the room, all she said was, "Come on in,
your father and I have to talk to you."

"Not me," said Pop. "I don't have one damn thing
left to say."

5.

Your father and I have to talk to you.

Funny you should say that, I was just thinking the same thing.

Why did everything look so funny in that room?

Corny old record: "You'd better sit down, kids, and listen to meeee . . ."

Have to talk

Well we could talk about that party you dragged me out of, there was a girl there, not Welles, that I think I could have put my tongue inside her mouth, we would go behind the curtains in the auditorium, so Welles wouldn't see.

Why was Pop dangling like a paper skeleton and why

was Mom circling, poking and shoving at her little pile of crap and why wouldn't either of them look at me?

We could talk about why they dragged me home from all that just so I could watch them fight. Once I woke up in the middle of the night because the front door kept slamming: Thunk. Everybody in for the night. Thunk. Wait a minute, there it goes again. I went downstairs and there they were coming in from a party, they weren't even drunk: her on one side, trying to get the door open, him on the other, trying to get it shut. It didn't make any sense because none of us knew what they were doing, really, except sawing at each other. They both looked at me with Disney grins. "Oh hello, Freddy, we were just having a fight."

They looked terrible, marshmallow skin around the eyes; their mouths were blurred like the little girl's in the vampire movie, she looks up at you from this arm she's chewing on, her father's, I think. We kept shuffling: Mom next to me, him next to me, him next to her for a second, it was an accident, oh excuse me, springing away. Nobody knew what to say. Nobody could figure out where to stand or what to do.

She was reminding us, Pop especially. "Your *father* and I have to talk to you."

"Mom?"

I was swallowing lead. Cheer up, maybe somebody only died. Maybe it's just another, you know, Fact of Life, they left it out by accident or it was too heavy for the main lecture so they saved it up until you got older. Maybe they're only going to send you to boarding school.

"Not we, Nina. You." Pop looked over my head at

her. "You're the one that has to talk to him, Nina, you're the one that's going."

"I think you have more to explain."

I was trying to pull things into a shape I could manage. "I was at a fucking *party*."

Pop snapped. "Don't use that word in this house."

"Fred, your father has something to tell you."

"Your mother has something to tell you."

"Not me, you."

"Dammit, Nina."

"Can I go to bed?"

They didn't even hear me. Pop was saying, "All right, take off without any explanations. That'll show me."

I thought she was going to hit him. "This doesn't have anything to do with you."

They were backing farther and farther apart; if they were choosing teams neither one of them had called on me and I didn't know where I was supposed to stand.

"If it's not us, what is it?"

She shook her head. "I don't know."

"Then why are you doing this to us?"

Score one, Pop.

"Not to you." She had a look I had never seen before, half nightmare, half figurehead. "For me."

"But I love you." We had been jockeying and by this time he had managed to snag me, pretending I needed him to put his arm around me so we could lean together. "Freddy loves you."

"Well I love you too." She jammed her dumb little purse in her pocket and tried to loop her arm through the strap on my pack.

"Then why don't you stay?"

"Mom, that side is broken."

"You know damn well I can't stay." It snapped and she groaned and tried the other side.

"You were going to sew it. Mom."

"Well I got busy." She got it as far as her elbow and then tried for the blanket roll and got that under the arm. She was wrestling with the easel too but there was no way that she was going to manage the suitcase without losing everything.

"Nina, why are you doing this to us?"

The blanket roll was coming unsnailed and sliding out of itself. "Mom."

She gave up on the pack strap and put down the easel and got the pack under the other arm. I don't know what she was going to do about the suitcase or the blanket roll that was starting to trail, she was kicking and pushing at all that junk getting redder and madder, her hair was wild and her face was flaming, I don't know whether it was all that stuff she had to handle that she was mad at or herself for not being able to do it or whether it was us, she whipped around and yelled: "I'm doing it because I have to. Now will you shut up?"

But he wouldn't. "At least tell me where you're going."

I thought she was going to throw the pack at him. "You still haven't figured it out?"

"Nina, I don't want to."

"I already told you, I'm going to the MBTA."

"Oh for God's sake, Nina." Pop stepped over and took the pack from her and helped her get a better grip on the easel. I tightened the bedroll for her, the trouble was the nylon was too slippery, and after I got it together I

stuffed it under her arm, I could hear Pop's voice, rag-
gedy but intolerably patient: "Wherever you're going,
I'll drive you."

Where was I and what was I doing? Was I out of it and
why? That was me down there in our driveway with the
shiteating smile helping her to get her stuff into the
back seat, it was like sending the kittens off to the gas
chamber, nobody wants it but it's something you have
to do. There I was moving the suitcase to make room
for the pack and after that I had to help Pop fold up the
easel so he could get it into the trunk, a bad scene from
the bio lab, why won't this damn corpse *bend*, Mom and
I stood around in the driveway while he tucked in the
arms and legs and got the trunk shut, some of us were
trying not to cry and the rest of us were looking like
somebody I didn't even know. After he got the trunk
shut she was just going to get in the car and ride away
and I hadn't even tried.

"Mom, wait a minute. Mom."

"It's all right, Freddy, I love you."

Pop was getting in the car on his side.

"Then how about explaining?"

He had the motor running, he was gunning it like he
could hardly wait.

"I can't, your father's waiting."

"He doesn't really want to."

"I'm sorry, I have to go." She stood there in the cold
air with the dark around her and I guess she remembered what she was supposed to do; she gave me a quick
hug. I could smell her, all the things she used to keep
her hair smooth and her face nice and her pits from
smelling, and then I was standing there by myself with

that perfume on me and my hands still falling and the two of them were gone.

I figured I would go in and break up all her stuff, that would show her, but then I figured if she had left it behind, she didn't care about it anyway. I poured the perfume down the toilet all the same and then I went downstairs and took a snort of Galliano from the Christmas bottle they had never opened, it was so gucky that I couldn't even get drunk. Pop came back. When I heard the brakes squeaking I went to the back door and sprang out, Gotcha. I suppose I was yelling.

"What the hell was that for, Pop, what was it for?"

"I just took her. She said tell you to remember your history paper."

"Where did you take her?"

"I took her down there." Then he puffed up so he could get together enough air to make some noise. "Your mother . . ." His voice came out high and thin, the way it does when you breathe helium. "Your mother is going down to Cambridge to stay with a friend."

"Well what for?"

"Sometimes people have to be—apart."

"I suppose you're going to try and tell me it's a sick friend."

"I'm not going to try and tell you anything." He looked worse than I had ever seen him but if he was going to cry he wasn't about to let me see him, he said, "How can I tell you when I don't even know?"

6.

WHEN I GOT to school the next day nobody even noticed. They were all talking about Farter. I got there late because Pop and I both slept through the alarm, we didn't want to be awake again, ever. When we did get up we had coffee together, we sat in the middle of last night's dishes without saying much and then he drove me to school before his ten o'clock class. It turned out Farter was suspended for mooning in the girls' bathroom, he probably would have gotten away with it except Mrs. Estabrook was in there making a head check when he popped in the door, she was laughing so hard Farter got scared and popped back out without zipping up and Mr. Runcible caught him. Nobody said anything about me coming in late but I had the idea that was why they were all whispering, and those were things about my mother that they were writing and folding in funny shapes to pass down the row. Then I found out about Farter and I thought wow, maybe that would keep their minds off it and they would never have to know. Mom was never very big on P.T.O. or going to things I was in anyway, if I didn't mention it then maybe they wouldn't either and if my folks didn't get back together then maybe at least I could make her come to my high school graduation, if she didn't it wouldn't matter because by that time I would be leaving for college and I would never have to face any of them.

I got through the day all right but it was hard. I kept my head down so they wouldn't see me. In Jack London or the *National Geographic* there is this thing about the pack eating the wounded animal, I was scared to death some kid would catch me licking a sore and wham, they would be all over me. I was swallowing hard but the thing kept getting bigger and bigger, I was swelled up with it, pretty soon I would start changing color, gangrene, which as much as anything explains why I threw up in Phys Ed. I did it behind the bleachers but when I got wiped off and fell back in line Coach Short made a face and sent me to the nurse. Another day he probably would have kept me there doing push-ups because he thinks if you can just do enough pushups or run the right number of laps he can make a man of you, but I guess he saw I was beyond it. I was going to walk home but she was taking some kid to the emergency room with a busted lip so she dropped me off. At the door she said, "Is there anybody here to take care of you?" and I said "Yes Ma'am my mother will do it," and for a crazy minute I thought it would be true, that she, you know, Did It To Bring Us To Our Senses, maybe now I would change my ways and start making my bed. There wasn't anybody, just the dirty dishes and on the stairs, my socks, it was empty minus, so I went to bed.

After school Welles came. I heard her banging on the door and when she wouldn't go away I stuck my head out.

"Go away."

"I brought your books."

"You can give them to me on the bus."

"Mrs. Estabrook is having a test."

"I don't care."

"But I brought your book."

"Leave it on the porch."

"It's raining."

"I don't care." I slammed the window down but she didn't go away.

The next thing was, she rang the bell.

I thought if I didn't go down she would give up after a while so I waited and after ten minutes I went down far enough so I could see through the glass alongside the door. She was still standing there, getting wet. I thought, Serves her right, and I would have left her there except she saw me and I had to let her in.

She was mad as hell. "What's the matter with you?"

"Nothing."

"Bullshit." She wasn't looking at me, exactly, she was looking at the stuff lying around, she dodged past me so she could see down the hall to our kitchen. "What happened?"

"Nothing, now will you give me the book and go home?"

She was already on her way to get something to eat.

She shoved the book on our kitchen table, I think she put it down in the dried egg on purpose, and stood with her head inside the refrigerator, looking for something we didn't seem to have.

"Is this your *food?*"

"What's the matter with it?"

"Leftovers, and half of it stinks." She took a Coke and slammed the **door**.

"Well tough."

"That's not what I mean." She was looking for a glass because she hates drinking out of the can. "It's OK, Mom says she won't make it through the week."

"What?"

"Your mother. This guy is a marriage counselor and a jerk."

"A *marriage* counselor."

"Not really. He was a Psych major in college, he just set himself up in business. My mother says there's a lot of money in it, people who don't know what they're doing always go to people who don't know what they're talking about. Is this the last clean glass you *have?*"

"She didn't say anything about a marriage counselor."

"He teaches Psych in night school."

I couldn't decide if I wanted to hit Welles or find this marriage counselor, or whatever he was, and blow him up. "She said she had to find herself."

"Oh, that. That's what they all say." Welles could see I was getting mad, she said, "You want to hit me or break something?"

I just kicked the table. "It wouldn't do any good. I'm going to be cool."

"You want to come over to my house?"

"Your mother already . . ."

"Everybody does."

"Shit."

"We could make toll house cookies or something."

"Fuck."

"You might as well, your Pop is coming to dinner."

"Oh shit."

"They'll only come and get you."

"Shit shit."

"Are you coming or do you want me to go away?" She was getting ready to go, she was on her way into the hall and I was scared to death she would leave without me so I would be stuck there for the rest of the day, I would have to eat beans out of the can and then sit around in the mess and hold my hands.

"Yeah. Shit. OK."

"It's going to be all right," she said from the hall, where I couldn't see her. "I mean, it happens to so many kids that nobody even notices."

"That's what you think." I could hear my voice seesawing so I thought I'd better quit talking.

She got busy with her coat so she wouldn't have to look at me; she was hanging it over her head to keep off the rain. She kept talking from underneath the coat. "My mother said this one thing I was supposed to tell you. She said no matter what they make you think, it wasn't you." She busted out the door and ran.

I busted out after her, I was in a hurry to get into the rain.

Her coat fell off and she was out in the middle of the street swinging her arms. "Fartface."

"What?"

"You forgot your stupid coat."

"Up yours."

"Same to you."

"Dumbhead."

"Bunghole." She was yelling; she picked up the coat and swung it at me, we were both jerking around in the rain haw-hawing, at least our voices were going up and down but I don't think we either of us knew then what it was from.

"Creep."

"Dork."

Good old Welles, if I had never met you I would want to put my hands under there and find out about you but we were little together, we have to be people we can trust. "Spaz."

"Shithead."

I was laughing and gargling rain.

"Yeah, you. You—pissant."

Finally a car came along and almost ran over us so we had to move.

Pop and I were kind of embarrassed to run into each other at Welles's house, it was, Well, fancy meeting you here, or, You of all people, hem hem, Father, Son, Father; I was feeling naked because I had thought what happened to us was, um, Our Secret, and there he was with them finishing their martinis, they knew more than I did, and there I was with Welles, which meant she knew; I had been all squinched up thinking if we could just keep this a secret then maybe it would turn out not to be true, but they were sitting around with their legs over the chair-arms, looking rumpled and used, so I suppose Pop had Told All. I wonder what they thought when he told about loading her stuff in the car after she made her Farewell Address, the stupid asshole just tied up the trunk so her easel wouldn't fall out and drove her

wherever it was she thought she was going. In the
movies they used to chain Larry Talbot to the bedpost
until he got over the change, later on he would be sorry
as hell for all the trouble he caused them; why hadn't
Pop? Why wasn't he trashing the living room or yelling
into the phone, and if he couldn't even do that why
wasn't he tearing his hair or gouging his eyes out with
his face ripped and the sockets bleeding, didn't he give
a shit. Why—

Mrs. Welles said, "Dinner."

When we all sat down together it was a lot like being
in *The Waltons*, we were this huge family. I have never
sat down with that many people except at Christmas or
Thanksgiving but they do it every night, and they never
run out of things to say; at the end there Mom and Pop
and I used to watch the TV while we were eating just to
fill up the silence. We looked so nice, I wanted us to be
nice, they were but I was still T. Rantula, hanging over
my plate with a new set of pictures flashing behind my
eyes: her and that marriage counselor, them naked,
whatever they did together, white flanks against white
flanks with curly hair mixing, I was on fire with it, eaten
up from the insides out and when I looked up and
found them still talking, something they had just said
snagged all the ugly pictures I had just made and
dragged them along behind it

What

something something Haskell Tilghman

What the

dragged me along too so I said:

"What about Mr. Tilghman?"

Welles snapped around to look at me, I guess she

hadn't been listening either, and Pop said "Nothing" too fast.

What.

Mr. Welles said, "Nothing," Mrs. Welles wanted to know didn't we have any homework and had I had enough spaghetti, they wouldn't quit changing the subject and the next thing I knew Pop was thanking them and getting up to go.

Something about Mr. Tilghman.

". . . a lot to do at home. Right, Fred?"

I stayed where I was. There was nobody home and I didn't want to go. Maybe they would answer my question. Their house was warm, they had a mother and a father home.

"Fred?" Pop was standing by my chair, trying to lift me with his voice; it is the tone Coach gets when he is trying to get me to do something we both know is impossible. I stayed where I was until the silence got so awful that I had to look at him.

Mrs. Welles said, "He's welcome to sleep here."

"Hey Futch, why don't you?"

"I thought we would . . ." Pop didn't go on, he just turned around to look me in the eye; it wasn't that we had to leave right now or that we had anything to do after we got home, it was that he had to find out whether I was with him, whether we were going to be able to keep it going.

Mrs. Welles said, "It's no trouble, really."

Welles said, "Futch?"

I was looking at all the lines in Pop's face, the way the rest of him drooped, down to those dangling hands, and I knew if I wanted to stay he wouldn't stop me so I had to go. "Thanks a lot, but we've really got to . . ." I looked at Pop and he was so glad, I couldn't finish. I just got up and we thanked them and went off together: us two.

He didn't say anything but I could feel his whole weight on me.

When we got to our house it was all dark and I thought Oh God I don't want to go in there but Pop had us both out of the car before I could think about it and when we went inside he turned on all the lights and it was the craziest thing, he started picking up all the newspapers and fluffing the pillows the way he does when there is somebody coming to the house.

"Let's don't live like pigs while she's away, OK?"

"What difference does it make?"

I guess he must have seen some of the stuff flashing behind my eyes: all those dirty pictures, because he said, "Do you want to talk about it?"

I could see he didn't really want to hear it so I blanked my eyes to shut the pictures away from him.

He wouldn't quit. "Do you want to tell me how you feel?"

"I feel fine."

God he was trying. "You might feel better if we talk about it. Freddy?"

Freddy might. Not T. Rantula, who cannot be hurt. "Pop, what's the matter with Mr. Tilghman?"

He said, "I know it's hard for you to understand, but I want you to know it wasn't you she was leaving behind, it was me. OK?"

Why the fuck did you let her go? I didn't say anything.

He said, "We love her and we want her to be happy, right?"

Right, hell. "You didn't answer my question."

He said, "Meanwhile, we're going to have to keep it together, right?" He handed me a couple of ashtrays to empty; he would keep holding them out until I took them from him; he would stand there holding them out and staring at me until I said what he wanted. "OK?"

"Whatever you say, Pop." I went to empty them.

7.

I HUNG AROUND Welles's house a lot, I needed to keep warm and they were doing a pretty good job of it, I couldn't get enough. There was nothing much left at our house except me and Pop bumping into each other with those ashtrays, the morning papers, the mail: grins that were just teeth, God were we ever cheerful, we were so hearty it made you want to puke, and the whole time we were trying to figure out which one of us we had to thank for the whole thing: Not it, Fred. Well me neither, Pop. Not it. The food was OK, Pop knocked himself out making meat loafs and tricky casseroles, but he could never remember what else you were supposed to do and I couldn't either, so we had a whole gang of meals that were one weird dish without any salad or dessert, we drank milk out of the carton and ignored the lettuce until it turned black and we had to throw it out. Pop kept coming around corners saying, Nina? and half the time he forgot to turn out the lights. For the time being he was not so good, so mornings I would climb into my T. Rantula suit and sit across the breakfast table slupping cornflakes while he drank his coffee and told me about his dreams, I could hardly wait to be out stepping over entire cities on my eight springy legs, I would knock over buildings in Cambridge until I found out where Mom was; then I would open her room like a nutshell and lift her out with two hairy pincers; I would knock over this marriage counselor and sink my fangs into him, he would be poisoned where he lay.

I said to Pop, "You never said anything about a marriage counselor."

Pop said, "That stuff is a crock, Freddy, you can't counsel marriage."

"That's not the point."

"It either is or it isn't," Pop said.

"You never told me there was a guy."

"Well the guy is only part of it, I didn't think it was important."

"Bullshit."

He looked so sweet, sad, patient, why wasn't he out there shaking cities and messing up? "She left to find out who she is."

"She's my damn mother."

"That isn't enough."

"Then she can go to hell."

He would be trying to take my mind off it. "Listen, Fred, I had the craziest dream."

He only told me his dreams about the one thing; there

we were with her gone, maybe she had packed off with his balls because this was all he could dream about, he couldn't even dream any terrific ladies to chase or that would chase him, or if he did he wasn't about to tell me.

Here are some of Pop's dreams.

He is supposed to take a French test in college but he hasn't been to class ever. If he doesn't pass he can't graduate and get married but here it is the day of the test, they are handing out the exam papers and he doesn't even have a book.

He is standing up in front of his Donne class and they are waiting for him to begin. His mouth opens and nothing comes out but spit and air. They are still waiting. They will wait for the rest of his life.

Or he is at his best, he is doing his damndest when somebody gets up and starts yelling that this is all crap. Or else they start laughing. Or the only sound is all his students stampeding, his best lecture is drowned out by the sound of them stomping out. Or snoring.

He can't find the classroom.

He finds it but he can't get in.

Sometimes he is naked. Other times they are naked.

When he opens his mouth they start throwing things or else they chase him into the streets, if they catch him they will rip his heart out and tear it to bits.

He is struck deaf.

He is struck dumb.

He is struck dead.

My father, the *professor*.

I say, "Gee, Pop, that's terrible."

He says, "Every teacher dreams the same."

One of his students said, "Until I met you I thought professors were just like—*doctors*."

I wonder what doctors dream.

I was dreaming all the time too, asleep, awake, it was all the same after a while; I had nightmares about being trapped or threatened, escape dreams about green places where I was loved and happy until I had to wake up and swallow that loss along with the rest; I dreamed that Mom was calling, I would sit up in the dark saying, "What?" I had dreams I would be embarrassed to tell. In the daytime I was pretending I lived at Welles's house, I could bow my head at the supper table just like all their other kids; I dreamed I was T. Rantula onstage showing them, I would sing until my throat split and showed my true soul. There would be a zillion teenyboppers screaming and Mom up front in a box seat with a white fur cape on, she would be sitting with Pop in his tuxedo and she would be wearing a little rhinestone crown; I also slid into the body of the big T. Rantula, I was eighty feet tall and nothing could touch me, if anybody tried I would waste our school and everybody in it, I would smash the town hall if the spirit moved me and I would make Mom famous at whatever it was she wanted if only she would come back, I would hire her an art gallery or an opera house, the way they did in *Citizen Kane*.

I had wet dreams, dry dreams, fright dreams, daydreams, to the outside world I might look like any other kid just going along, but these things kept slipping in to change me and I knew there was more piling up in the back of my head just waiting for me to cork off at night so it could move in and take over. I hung out with Welles a lot and hung around their house a lot, she hadn't changed but I had and it made me guilty, I was so dark and mean that I would look over at her smiling

and think maybe I should smash her one just to bring
her to her senses: *You, what do you know about what
I am.* Then one night I looked at her parents trying to
be nice to me and I thought they would be shocked if
they could see inside my head; I was having a hard time
swallowing because of the sprouting venom sacs and the
fangs already popping, there were black hairs springing
out on my ankles and the backs of my hands, I was all
ready to turn into God knows what at the next full
moon and there they were smiling and understanding,
boy were they ever understanding, when I already knew
nobody outside could have any idea what it was really
like; they had opened up their family for me and I was
about to poison it so I thanked them and got up and
left. I went over to Tig's.

You see, we always gather at the full moon;
Misery loves.

That isn't it either. What my grandmother always said
was: Like attracts like, but if that was true, why was I
going over there? I would rather die than be like that.

When he opened the door they were still having dinner
and for a minute I thought I had made a mistake, the
Tilghmans were sitting with their heads bent under the
fake candlelight and they both turned smooth smiles
toward the door before they even saw it was me. Then I
looked at Tig and we knew each other, I didn't have to
look for the black hairs hanging out of his sleeves. He
was relieved to see me, he said, "Hey, Futch." I guess I
was getting him out of something. "Futch."

I said, "Hi Tig. I."

He cut his eyes around at the two of them and then
said to me, through his teeth, "Maybe not now, OK?"

But his mother was already falling out of her chair waving at me.

"Fred. Fred Crandall, come on in."

"Thanks Mrs. Tilghman, I."

"Fred, come and eat something, it's all Tig's favorites and he's hardly . . ."

"I just ate."

She kept on talking, you would think she had run into me at a cocktail party. "In the name of heaven come and have some cake."

She sounded so anxious that I did go in, I even had a second piece because Tig didn't want his, he said he was in training, they were about to start in on him about that but I was there so they had to let him alone. Mr. Tilghman's mouth was smiling but he had a deep line in between his eyebrows where he hadn't managed to un-scowl, so I guess they had been having a fight. He and Mrs. Tilghman were knocking themselves out being charming, God are they polite. After a while Tig asked if we could be excused, I was never so glad to get away from a table in my life.

In the kitchen Tig said, "Want to blow up my parents?"

"We could get Danny's chemicals."

"We could pin it on him."

"Nah, they'd know it was us. You want to spend the rest of your life in jail?"

"This is jail," Tig said. "We could run away."

"If we left a ransom note we might get rich." I was already thinking about Pop, waiting for me at the window. "Where would you go?"

"Desert island, maybe, maybe Florida."

"We could get a houseboat and live on the river." The way my father said he did.

"Someplace with no people. When we got there I would just lie around until I sank into the sand." Tig was jittering in one spot; he couldn't keep still but he couldn't get going either.

"Let's do something, let's get out of here."

"OK, OK."

"We could go and spy at Farter's." I went to the door, thinking he was going to come with me. "Maybe they're having pot."

"Or we could sneak into the movies."

"Are you coming?"

He still hadn't moved. "I can't."

"Why not?"

"I'd really like to but I can't." The parents were rattling dishes in the dining room; Tig looked at me, at the back door, at the swinging door to the dining room, in a minute they would push through and find us but he still couldn't move, it was spooky. "I have to stay here, I'm in training."

"For God's *sake*."

"Do you want to see my place?"

Mr. Tilghman was coming through the swinging door, creep, I didn't want to have to see him, so when Tig headed for the cellar I headed after Tig. We got the door closed just as his father called him, so we could pretend we didn't hear.

Tig had fixed up the playroom since I was down there last, all the kid stuff had been pushed out of the way, stuffed animals lying around in corners and the Ping-Pong table with the Space Walk on it shoved back in the shadows; there was a trapeze and a chinning bar and he had a wrestling mat and weights and over in one corner a straw mat with an alarm clock next to it, there was a wooden pillow at the head, like Japanese wrestlers have, and I said, "Is this where you *sleep?*"

"If you can sleep there you can sleep anywhere." Tig was looking kind of proud and anxious. "Well what do you think?"

"What's it all for?"

"I'm in training all the time now."

"Gee, Tig, it doesn't look too comfortable."

"I suppose you think prison camps are comfortable? Or capitalist jails?"

"What does that have to do with it?"

"I want to be ready."

"Ready for what?"

He said, "I just want to be ready, that's all."

"I don't get it."

He sat down on the wrestling mat with his knees up under his chin. "It's all crap, Futch, I'm tired of taking all this crap, they give it to us because they figure what do we know, we're only stupid kids, but just because you're a kid doesn't mean you have to be weak. Do you know I do a hundred push-ups every night?"

"Gee that's great."

"The trouble with us is, we're all out of condition, look at you, you're in terrible shape, and me, gross, look at all this ugly flab." He punched himself in the ribcage; it was like a washboard under his shirt. "We're out of shape so the first little thing that comes along, it knocks us flat."

I was running my tongue behind my back teeth, feeling for the bumps where the fangs were coming up. "Maybe you're right."

"We're all too soft." He looked like he was about to cry. "We're all so fucking soft."

"I guess that's a problem."

Tig was shaking himself, trying to pull himself back. "Look, Futch, I'm sorry about your mother and everything."

"It's nothing."

"If you got yourself in shape it might help."

If that was what it did to you I didn't want it. "Yeah, right."

"I don't know what's the matter with them."

I didn't try to ask him what he meant. His were there together in the dining room all right, with their china faces in the pretend candlelight, they were together in the kitchen now, scraping leftovers off the plates, but here was Tig fighting hard to keep the black hairs from showing, he was pressing down on the bulges in his gums. I said, "You have a really neat setup here."

"Do you like it?"

"It's really great."

"I, uh, thought you ought to see it. When I heard about your mother and all?"

"It's nothing."

"I just thought, if you started working out."

"I don't think so, Tig."

"No kidding," Tig said. "It really makes a difference. Look at me."

He looked terrible. "You look great."

"Not yet, but I'm getting there. I get up at four-thirty to do isometrics, at six-thirty I go out to the track, the thing is, if I can only get myself in shape, then maybe the rest of it . . ."

"Yeah, Tig. Right."

"God, I hate my parents." For a minute he sounded like the old Tig but then he pulled himself together and clenched his jaw. "See, that's what I mean. That kind of thing."

"You mean saying what you think?"

"I've got to get it under control."

"Lord, Tig, let's go somewhere. I'll take you to the Dairy Queen, or we could go rolling on the hill."

Tig said, "We could get Welles and spy on Farter's house."

"Right. Let's go."

"I can't. I've got to get in shape." Before he could change his mind he flopped on the mat and started doing push-ups. "If you aren't going to work out, I guess you'd better go."

"Yeah, Tig. Right." I stood there for another minute to see if he was going to change his mind, I wanted to change his mind for him but he must have been up to fifty by that time, he wasn't even sweating.

"See you, Tig."

"Hey Futch."

"Yeah."

"If you ever want to use the weights or anything, you're welcome."

"Right."

"Maybe you'll come around again?"

"Sure, Tig. Now that I know where you are."

"If you ever get up early, maybe we could run together."

"After you get in shape maybe we can go to the movies or something. It's getting warm so we could take our bikes."

"I'd really like to." He sat up on the mat for a minute

and I could see he'd really like to, but what he reminded me of was Farter's dog that he used to keep chained to the tree out back, it always used to try and follow me but it never could because of being chained to the tree. There was no reason I could see but Tig couldn't cut loose, he couldn't follow even if he wanted to because he was tied there, he was going to go on doing push-ups even though there wasn't any chain.

I said, "Maybe tomorrow?"

"Maybe tomorrow," he said, even though we both knew he wouldn't. "And you'll come back and work out with me?"

"Next time, for sure."

"Any time, day or night."

"Right, Tig." I started up the stairs.

"Remember, any time."

His mother stopped me on the way out, I think she wanted to ask me a couple of hundred questions but all she did was say thank you for coming, she was certainly glad I had enjoyed the cake. The truly strange thing was that after I got out I felt a lot better, I could have been Mr. Terrific, compared to that bunch, both of his parents look like models for vodka ads or the sexiest new car, their house is full of paintings and antiques, even that cake was almost as good as it looked but leaving there was like getting out of the House of Usher right before the fall, I could hardly wait to get back to typical Pop in our average American home.

I went back the next night and the car was gone, I thought if his folks weren't home I might be able to pry him off the mat and take him out with me but it was good I didn't ring the bell because it was Tig that was gone and his father was there. I came through the woods alongside the house and there he was in his study with this student sitting alongside him at the desk, they were smoking and going over some papers, zzz, boring, I would have left but there was this strange thing. I couldn't really see because of the desk but it looked like Mr. Tilghman started tickling him, there was this great big grownup going tiggy, tiggy, he was just about to give this guy a vampire bite in the middle the way Pop did when I was little, and the guy must have thought it was strange too because he got up in a hurry and by the time he came out the front door he was running almost as fast as Tig. There was Tig's father on the step with his fists on his belt, staring out; I was scared he would catch me so I left.

8.

MOM WANTED TO SEE ME after all. She called up about her portable typewriter, that she had forgotten to take when she took her clothes and her Psych notes and my picture and her paints. She said Al was so busy she couldn't get him to drive her out to pick it up and Pop promised he would bring it in to Cambridge in the car along with me, he was going to drop me off at the corner with the typewriter and let me walk the rest of the way to spare them any embarrassment: Al and Pop coming face to face and not having anything to say, Mom and Pop coming face to face with too much to say, looking at each other over my head.

I said, "Why the hell shouldn't they be embarrassed? This whole thing is embarrassing."

"Try to think about my feelings."

"I am thinking about your feelings. Why don't you go and punch him up?"

"When you're older you'll understand."

"I don't know what I'm supposed to understand."

"For one thing, he's a decent guy."

"You mean you know him?"

"That's a different story."

"Well I hate his guts."

"Let's put it this way, Freddy, the more you fight it now the worse it's going to be later. Depending how things turn out you might have to learn to get along with Al."

"I'd rather die. I hate him."

"You don't even know him."

"I said, I hate him. Don't you hate him?"

Pop wouldn't look at me, he said, "Hatred doesn't have anything to do with it. What good would it really do if I went in and punched him up?"

"We would both feel better."

"It wouldn't make her any different. You have to let people be what they want to be. Right now . . ." He cleared his throat and looked miserable. "Right now your mother thinks she wants to be with Al." He had tried so hard to explain that he really thought he had done it, that he had made me understand and we were going to be pals some more. He couldn't stop looking at me, I don't know what he saw but he put his hand on my shoulder. "OK, Fred? OK?"

"Yeah, Pop." I thought I would open a little wider and let him see the fangs but I knew I'd better not. "Sure, Pop. Sure."

All the way down there in the car I planned what I

would do. I would say something that would wreck this guy or else I could smash him in the belly. If he was big enough he would beat up on me and there would be Mom, carrying my battered body back to our house, thinking up ways to explain it to Pop; I would bleed on her to get her attention and then I would wink: *Look what you did.* Maybe I would bust in on Al with one of his patients and prove he was a liar and a cheat and the patient and I could go and get the cops. After they took him to the station I would jump on his tape recorder and break the glass on his THIMK sign and then I would pee in all his files. I guess Pop was thinking some of the same things because he was driving the car like a Dodgem and by the time we got to the corner near the house his mouth was so tight that he could hardly pry it open to tell me which one it was, and when he reached over into the back to get the typewriter I could see he had the shakes. All he said was, "Be decent to her." Then he let me out.

If Al was even there I didn't get to see him. Mom must have been waiting just behind the frosted glass because she popped the door open before I even hit the steps. She pulled me inside and took the typewriter. I was trying to see past her into the rest of the house, where was he I was going to kill him, but she pushed the typewriter under a table and hugged me; I had to jump away because she didn't smell like perfume or Pit Stop or any of the usual things, she had a ponk that I had only ever noticed on Ida Cade at school, it was like hugging somebody that has come back from a long time in a strange country and I pulled away partly because it drew me for reasons I didn't want to think about. We stood and looked at each other for a minute; she was shaky and I thought, All *right.*

"Thanks for bringing the typewriter, we're into this project now and I couldn't get along without it."

I said, "Hi, Mom."

She said, "Well, Fred, how have you been?"

"Mom . . ."

"You're not a kid any more, Fred, we're just people together. I think you ought to call me Nina."

I said, "OK."

"Have you been all right?"

"I guess so."

"Are you getting enough vegetables?"

"I don't know." Who cares? Why don't you come back and see?

"And you're all right?" She was looking at me looking at her. She couldn't think of anything else to say. "You're all right?"

What was I supposed to say?

"Well." Her laugh was shaky, her just-before-the-party laugh, I was a guest and she was scared. "What would you like to do today?"

"I don't know."

"I have a friend who has an art exhibit . . ."

"Oh."

"I thought maybe you would like to look at somebody else's paintings for a change."

"I don't care."

"Or we could go over to the Harvard Coop, I'll buy you all the Ray Bradbury you can carry."

"I'm finished reading him."

"OK, I'll get you a new record."

That I would have liked. "No thanks, I . . ."

"They get all the new releases." She was getting desperate, like, what was she going to do with me now that she had to entertain me, me that we'd always known each other and just sort of hung out together no matter where we were and she'd never had to give a second thought. "What was the name of that singer you liked?"

Fangs. (You're welcome.) "T. Rantula."

Her mouth made a wavy line. "I'll get you the new T. Rantula."

"I already have it."

"Clothes, then. Lord knows you need a new jacket."

"I don't want a new jacket, Mom." Maybe I could make her cry.

"You must want *something.*"

I could hear somebody moving upstairs, they were out in the hall and about to come down. Maybe I could make her cry in front of this other person. "I don't care."

"That's *enough.*" I was never so surprised. She put her knuckles into my neck just the way she did when I was little, I guess she had me by the collar and she pushed me out the door.

The only thing we could think of that we both wanted to do was eat, so we ended up in this place off Harvard Square with round tables and brown air, they had beer in pitchers and it was an off-hour so we sat in a corner for a long time, just her and me, and after we talked about what we were going to eat and it came, we talked about what we were eating, I kept looking at her across from me and I just couldn't make any sense out of it, she looked the same but there was more to her; she had parts that I didn't know. Finally I said, *"Marriage* counselor."

"He's a teacher first, the other is only on the side."

"It's so corny."

"Fred, it's not anything like you think. I've known Al

a long time and so have you, you were just too little to remember. When things get a little easier I want you to meet him because you will really like him, in a way you're a lot alike."

"What do you mean, you knew him when I was little?"

"Didn't your father tell you?"

"Tell me what?"

"He was one of his first students."

"*Student.* Gross."

"Student *then.*" She had the knuckles look: look here, son, no fooling around. "Al is thirty-three."

"Student."

"Well I'm the student now. He turned out to be teaching at the community college and when I started classes . . ."

"Classes, you mean all that time you were going out to classes . . ." I couldn't stop the pictures flashing: naked people making pretzels of themselves.

"I was going out to classes," she said, being firm. The look meant shut up.

"Yeah, big deal." I didn't want any more of my lunch.

She finished her lunch and started on my french fries. I think she saw I wasn't eating but she couldn't make me because one word would put her back at the old stand, scraping baby spinach off my face and back into my mouth or standing over the eggplant casserole. She stood it as long as she could and then she said, "Don't you want to know why we need the typewriter?"

"Not really."

"I have a friend in the house. Angel. She used to work for a newspaper and we're writing a play. If you come and see it when it's finished maybe it will help you understand."

"I don't want to understand."

Her face went funny. "Oh Freddy I'd feel so right about everything if it weren't for you."

My friends call me Futch.

"Freddy?"

"I'm OK."

"Are you?" Her face was starting to look like those pink paper things they put around cupcakes.

So I told her what she wanted. "Sure."

"Oh Freddy. I wish you could come and stay with me and never have to go to school, we could be friends and just do what we wanted, I want you to come and meet them—there are some really beautiful people in the house."

"Oh." If she was supposed to be one I didn't know if that was what I wanted. Her hair was dirty and she smelled like somebody else, even from across the table; she had started looking like somebody else in dumb glasses and this sack thing she was wearing over the jeans, but she was looking straight at me now, which she hadn't done for a while, and she was talking to me more or less person to person instead of mother to kid. "What for?"

"They're my people now. It's where I belong."

I slipped. "I thought you belonged with us."

For a minute she blazed. "Who has the right to say where people belong?"

"Somebody has to."

"Not you. Not anybody else. I love you Fred, but I had to get out. My life was dripping away." She had me by the arm, grinding my wrist into the table, and I could feel her shaking. "All those years and nothing to show."

My wrist hurt and I tried to get loose. T. Rantula

would have knocked her out and dragged her home, knocking over tables in the restaurant and busting the door if he had to, to make way.

She was hanging on, trying hard to explain. "These last few years we were only pretending. We were just going through the motions."

I thought if she would just let go of my wrist I could handle it. "Oh," I said; anything to get free.

"I never got to what was underneath. The way I *was*."

I was thinking about the way I was: those black hairs, venom sacs bulging. "Maybe that isn't so bad."

"Even when we would go out together, the three of us, we weren't a family, we were somebody's idea of a family, magazine pictures, all I was was the middle-sized one that smiled at him when he wanted me to and held your hand so you wouldn't run into the street."

I could feel T. Rantula inside of me, he was rising up and shaking. I wrenched free. "Let go, you're hurting my wrist."

"Hold still, I'm trying to talk to you." Her face was going from pink to red, still crinkling, she kept going for my hand. "Freddy, try to understand."

"I'm trying." It's Futch, dammit.

"Let me have my life."

It was too late; T. Rantula was up on all eights by that time, banging on my insides with eight hairy elbows, busting at the part of me that held him in. I didn't know what I wanted to do about any of it: push her face into the cream pie she had ordered that was making her fat; set that house on fire and hide somewhere across the street where I could watch them running out like scorched ants; beat the living shit out of her and drag her back home where she belonged, or forget she was

my mother that had cut out on us, and move in with her
and Al and them. Yeah, if I didn't watch him T. might
be lured along by all the changes, we would pick up a
steel guitar and thirty-eight black suits with the jet and
silk fringe leggings and the sequins the size of water
beetles and move in with her even if she didn't want to
be my mother. I was swelling, getting uglier and uglier
and I thought: Pop. What is going to happen to me,
Futch, if I let her do this to Pop?

I could hear myself. "This Al."

"Yes?" She was scrabbling at my arm again, slobber-
ing because she thought she had convinced me.

So I had to look at her and say, "You two aren't
making it or anything," because I knew they were.

Score one for T. Rantula. I made her cry after all.

She cried for longer than she should have. She didn't
make any noise, it just came dribbling out over the leftover french fries and the cream pie that she had never
even touched because by that time she wasn't hungry
either. I felt terrible, she felt terrible and I knew she was
just going to sit there crying until I did something to
make her feel better, me that she had cut out on when
she cut out on Pop. I thought, after everything, why
should I, but I knew if I didn't we were going to be
there with her crying and me just sitting until about
midnight when the place closed and they finally kicked
us out. So I said, "Look, Mom, I really do want to see
your play when it gets finished."

"Really?"

"Pop too. We might even like it."

"Do you think he'll come?"

"He will if you ask him." I wanted to make her feel
better so I kept on. "Look, Mom, I've got to get home

pretty soon but another time I would love to come and meet everybody in the house."

"I hope you will." She took off the glasses so she could wipe her face and for a minute she looked more like herself. Her eyes kept on running but at least she was smiling. "Maybe neither of us could handle it today anyway. Look, Fred."

Oh Mom, why did you have to go and . . . "Yeah?"

"This play we're doing, I have to do. It may not explain anything but it's something I have to do, OK?" When I didn't say anything she said, "Look, I want you to tell your father—tell him this whole thing is something I have to do, OK?" She was begging again. "OK?"

So I said, "OK."

"OK." She put the glasses back on and paid and when we went back out into the street it was so bright it made us blind.

After that it was nice being with her. I thought she would put me on the MBTA but instead we went on walking. It was warm out, we were on the edge of spring and it was zoo time in Harvard Square. We wandered around with the rest, looking into store windows, and after a while I let her buy me an ice cream cone and I ate it while she smiled. I think we both felt pretty good; now that I had made her cry we were, yeah, free, because all the stuff that was between us was openly between us, she knew how I felt about most of it and we were going along together anyway. She poked me in the ribs and pointed. There was a cardinal in the middle of Harvard Square and we stood there in the street, looking up, until it went away. After that it started to rain and if we had been real people together, the way she wanted it, instead of mother and kid, she would have ignored the rain or we would have opened our coats and gone running into it, but instead she looked at me and made the slip, "You should have something on your head," so it turned out we weren't free after all, and when she put me on the MBTA nothing was resolved between us. I had seen her, I had seen the place but only the front hall and I hadn't seen Al at all; except for the part about the play there was nothing much I could tell Pop, she hadn't sent him any messages, there was no point him frisking me when I came in the front door or looking over my shoulder to see if she was following, lurking on the walk or stashed in a bush, because that was all there was. When I went down there I had thought there might be things we could do about it, her and me or me and Pop or Pop and her and me, but all I had done was let her buy me off with lunch and ice cream and there I was on the MBTA, headed for home.

9.

BY THE TIME I got to the other end I was too big and ugly to go home.

I hadn't figured out what to tell Pop. That she was all different? Didn't even ask about him? That I would pay for dinner out if he would drive because I couldn't stand sitting around the kitchen table one more night, two pale noodles with nothing to say but: What's new? Uh — ah — nothing. What's new with you? It was worse than that. I didn't want to look at him because his face was my face half the time now, I knew what was on it and I didn't want to see.

What I did instead was, I hung around the town center. Pop had given me walking-around money for Cambridge, that Mom hadn't let me spend, so I thought

I would go to zit city and buy eight pounds of chocolate or something plastic that I could break on the the way home but it turned out there wasn't anything I wanted. The only thing that looked halfway interesting was the lava lamps inside the specialty shop, I would never be able to afford even the little one. The one I wanted had a fake gold base, the stuff inside it was red and the other stuff in with the red looked green, really ugly; when it was plugged in the green stuff started to bubble and writhe and I wasn't sure just why I wanted to move in and live there except the green stuff looked the way I felt. By the time I quit watching it and started home it was getting dark.

When I got as far as Welles's house she came tearing down the walk, I guess she had been on the watch, waiting to spring out.

"Futch. Hey, Futch."

"Go away."

"Will you come *here?*"

"What's the matter?"

"I've got something. Come and see."

It was better than going home so I followed her around back to their garage. There was this carton with a lot of junk in it.

"What's that? It looks like garbage."

She was so pleased. "It is. I got it from Tilghman's house."

"You were in their garbage?"

"I was just walking by and it sort of fell out. I thought it might help us help Tig."

"I don't know what you mean."

"Yes you do."

She wasn't looking at the box, she was looking at me.

I nodded. "Right." It was the first time either of us had said out loud that there might be something the matter with Tig.

"I thought if we could get something on him he might stop."

"Who?"

"Tig's father."

Why did I get the dry swallows? "I don't know what you're talking about."

She faced off. "Yes you do. Whatever it is, that's why Tig." She was on her knees in front of the box, going through it like Nancy Drew or Harriet the Spy.

I couldn't quit swallowing. "What's he doing?"

"My parents said harassing students. That's all they would say." She looked up at me the way we used to when it was marbles instead of garbage. "I just thought we might get something on him. Help me sort this stuff, OK?"

So I got down next to her and started sorting through their garbage: old bills, lecture notes in the kind of writing they put on greeting cards, a Kotex box, orange peels, I don't know what she was looking for, a signed confession? Counterfeit plates? I didn't know what we were going to find. "I think this is dumb."

She was pushing. "We've got to do something."

We had to stop Tig running. "If you could tell me what you're looking for."

"I told you I don't know."

T. Rantula was nudging. I said, "We're not going to find it in here," but I kept on anyway, not because there was anything in her box of garbage but because she wanted me to and besides there was this other stuff in my mind, all sifting down, and it wasn't useless papers

and wrecked panty hose and letters stuck to moldy
food, it was something that gave me the dry swallows,
that I might already know, it went together with what
her parents said, there was a whole gang of pictures sort
ing themselves too fast for me to look at them, it wa
like shuffling a deck of cards without seeing the faces
they filled my head and I didn't want to turn them
over.

We went through everything twice. I started again, but
Welles was getting tired of it. "Oh all right, shit. Maybe
I made a mistake."

"I don't know." I was still crouching over the box; the
cards in my head were shuffling faster and faster.

"It's time for supper anyway."

Her mother was calling from the house.

She got up. "I've got to go in. If I find out anything
else I'll call you, OK?"

"Yeah, right." I didn't really hear. I was fighting down
this dirty feeling, I didn't even want to look at her, I
would be embarrassed to have her see me now. "So I'll
see you."

She wouldn't go away. "Are you going home or
what?"

I had to be alone to— "I said, I'll *see* you."

"Do you want to come in and have supper?"

"I can't."

"It's getting late."

I didn't look up but I knew she was still standing over
me. I could hardly wait to get rid of her but I didn't say
anything more and she didn't say anything.

Her mother called again.

"Look, it's probably nothing."

"Your mother wants you."

"So don't sweat it, OK?"

Why wouldn't she go? I said, "OK."

So I was alone in the garage after all, and I could stop pretending to look into the box. There was never anything in there except trash, we weren't going to find anything we could use on him, there might not be anything, I was only beginning to figure it out: what I saw that time, tiggy, tiggy, the vampire bite, it was . . . It was dark out but I couldn't make myself get up, my legs were cramped and I was cold but I kept on hunching over the box and then just when I thought I could stop it coming out without me wanting to it all snapped together, or flew apart; it was like shuffling the janitor's dirty playing cards that we had never let Welles see, except that was Mr. Tilghman naked in all those rubber poses, *harassing,* and the other face was blurry, scared, that student, others, it was so dirty, me; I felt guilty for knowing it; I was filthy, slimy in the armpits and the crotch and smarmy in the crack, I was glad Welles was gone because I didn't want her to have to know.

I got up fast, trying to outrun the pictures, and as soon as I got outside I felt better. I was going home and I kept thinking, I'll tell Pop. I guess I was thinking maybe he would tell me I had made a mistake, and I wouldn't have to do this; if it wasn't a mistake at least Pop would know what to do.

What did I think he was going to do, make everything all right? Go to the cops or our college president and get Mr. Tilghman fired? Call in the FBI or punch him up? None of the above. He didn't do anything. Not anything. His face changed about a hundred times while I was tell-

ing him but not one of the things on it was surprise, and
when I finished he just stood there. I couldn't stand it,
I started yelling. "What are you going to do?"

"I don't know. I don't have anything to go on."

"I just told you." Maybe I thought I had one last
chance. If he would deny it. I went fishing. "Or maybe I
was wrong. Like, it isn't true?"

He looked terrible, worse than he had the night Mom
went. "It's true. Look, Freddy, I don't want you to think
I haven't thought about it. I don't know what to do."

"You already knew?"

"How do I know what I knew? I wasn't there with
them, Freddy. I didn't see. These things are hard to
prove."

"But you already knew?"

He wouldn't look at me, he only nodded.

"You already knew and you didn't do anything?"

I thought he was going to cry. "What could I do?"

"Dammit to hell Pop you have got to stop him. You've
got to tell." There I was yelling again, I thought if I
yelled loud enough I would get him moving but he was
still just standing there with those great big useless
hands and I couldn't believe he would just let it go.

"Freddy, there are other people to think about."

"What about the ones he already hurt?"

He wouldn't budge. "It would kill Maida."

I could feel my face twisting, if I cried he would never
pay attention. "She can go to hell."

"These are never things all by themselves. You have to
think about the family." He wanted to touch me and I
wouldn't let him. "Freddy, think what this would do to
Tig."

"I think he already knows."

He didn't want to hear that. He was saying, "We've got to do what is best, we have to protect the three of them."

"You can't just let it, let him, let . . ." I had been doing OK but I couldn't help it, I just caved in and started crying like a helpless bastard, he was hugging me and saying yes yes, there there, he kept telling me it was going to be all right so I thought he was going to do something after all. But then I started listening and it turned out he was saying all those things but he was saying something else: you couldn't just take a man's life away from him, you couldn't wreck his family. I said I would like to wreck him good, I would like to push him off a mountain or drop him from a plane or run over his head with a semi and then go back and forth over it until you couldn't tell what was left, but I was only a kid and couldn't do anything. He was my father, that ought to know what to do, but all he could say was, you couldn't do anything right now without hurting somebody, these things took time, his contract would be up soon anyway, he would be going in two years.

I remember yelling, "Two *years*," but all he did was say, "Easy, Fred, easy," and keep on patting my back until I hit him and he let me go. By that time I was throwing up noise.

"You," I said when when I could breathe again. "You can't do anything."

"You can't just go out and waste somebody." He reached out, trying to keep me. "There are times when there's nothing you can do."

I was looking for something to hit him with. "Then you might as well be dead."

"Freddy, wait."

I got away because I couldn't stand to be around him, and ran out into the dark. I could hear him calling after me but I just slammed the door. I hit the bottom step with the black fringe growing on the backs of my arms and legs, it was shaking with every step I took.

If nobody else was going to do anything about it, T. Rantula would.

It was getting big, the ground was shaking under heavy spider steps. By the time I got down to the center my breath was only catching every couple of minutes: *huh*-uh, as far as the rest of the world was concerned it could have been hiccups and I had never been crying; my face was OK because I had washed it in the fountain at the MBTA.

I unzipped my jacket and went over to the specialty shop and ripped off the lava lamp, it wasn't hard, I didn't even feel bad about it. I kept it under my jacket until I got to Tilghman's house, their hundred-thousand-dollar house with the brick veneer and poodle bushes with their leaves clipped; that big dumb house was just squatting on the lot with all the windows tight and the trim just painted and the front porch glowing from those imitation gas lights that look like they came off the set of *Oliver Twist*, the place was just like Mr. Tilghman on the outside, everything buttoned-up and shiny as a picture in a magazine, too unreal to be any good at all, and nobody home; T. Rantula was going to have to split it like a melon, splattering brains like seeds. I thought about leaving a note: *T. Rantula is on to you.* I thought of hiding in the bushes until they came, then I would smash him with the lava lamp before he could put his key into the lock, with Mrs. Tilghman flapping and Tig looking at me right before he pitched in to help.

I was so full of poison I couldn't hold it, I was going to vomit in another minute and I couldn't wait; I couldn't think beyond hating him, so in the end I did the only thing I could, I took the lava lamp out of my front and lifted it over my head and smashed it on their front steps.

10.

I NEVER TOLD Welles. I came down to the bus stop
the next day thinking everything would have to be
changed by me knowing, like the forest after Snow
White gets lost: snarling bushes, maneating trees, but
there were the same old kids standing around on the
same old corner, nobody looked up when I came along
so I guess in spite of everything even I looked the same.
I don't know where Tig was, maybe he was going to
spring out of the bushes after the bus got us, so he could
run along in the street behind; either that or he was
already running the five miles to school, he would run
until his guts fell out if nobody stopped him, he would
be going along in his Adidas with his small intestine
streaming out behind. I didn't know if Welles was going
to see my face and start asking questions or what, I

thought maybe we could just forget the whole thing, or she could, I was trying to think how to take her mind off it when she just began.

"I told my parents what we were doing."

"You what?"

"You know. The garbage. They said for us to let it be."

The garbage. God. How much did they. I was shaking inside. I just held my breath and waited.

"They said something else."

I couldn't stop shaking, all my insides were rattling. "Never mind. Why don't we just."

"No." She was staring right at me. She wouldn't let go. "They said tell you it's not your fault."

"What?" My *God*, how could they . . .

"About them." She was looking at me with those level eyes, I could see right through them to the inside, and her inside was a lot better looking than mine. "You know."

"What?" I tried to unstop my ears. I didn't even know what she was talking about.

"The whole thing. Your folks."

"Oh, that." I wasn't even thinking about that. I didn't want her to see my insides, so I had to look away. "They said that before."

She wouldn't quit. She was still looking at me, I was scared to death she was going to look right into me and find out but all she said was, "Don't get mad. They just want you to be OK."

I was holding everything as tight as I could: what I knew, what that made of me; everything inside me was rubbing against everything else. She thought it was this other thing, but I knew . . .

"Futch?" She was waiting on me.

"Yeah."

"Be OK. OK?"

The thing was spreading out of hand . . . "Yeah, right, Welles. OK."

"Are you all right?"

"Of course I'm all right." *A bloodstain darkening our land* . . .

"If you want to, I'll go away." She was such a good friend she would do anything.

"No, it's all right." *The world was slipping into sand* . . . and my mother was down in Cambridge. I looked at Welles for a minute; she looked so clean, she could have been Dick Tracy's girl sidekick, or Lois Lane. Once she stood out in the rain for about four hours while I tried to get my father's old motorbike to start up again. This was the same kind of thing, no more. She was not going to have to know what Mr. Tilghman was doing, would believe what her parents told her, would never have to know. I knew because I was . . . what? *And I was howling along.*

"Look. Here comes the bus."

Rantula. Nobody came along to sing the backup. There was Welles smiling and thinking about something else, and Tig was running out of sight. If I couldn't stop him running, how could I expect to get my mother back?

These are the last days, the last days, the last . . .

And I could never trouble Welles with it because her insides were so much prettier than mine. I could not go back to Pop or even Mr. and Mrs. Welles because they might wonder what there was about me that caused all this ugliness. Grownups, they would just smile and try to keep things running along normally, so they could play business as usual, they would plant flowers to cover the shit. If they ignored it maybe it would go away, if they could pretend none of it was true then maybe none of it would have to be true. So there was going to be only one person left thinking about it: me.

At first I thought the sky had to fall right away. I thought the next time I looked at Mr. Tilghman he would crack down the middle like a lead soldier because he would know I knew or else I would split and die from knowing it. After that didn't happen I had to believe something would happen, somebody important would find out and fire him, he would crash out of the closet and give our ancient dean a soul kiss or rape some football player, they would find them behind the stands with blood on his fangs and the victim would sob out his story to the arresting officer, or else they would all be at some big party and that handsome asshole would forget himself and ask the coach to dance. I thought at least he would get hit by a truck. Nothing happened at all. Nothing was going to happen; now that I knew about it the big flashy cardboard bastard seemed to be all over the place, he went every place that Pop went, you could look in the window at any party and see him dancing with the glad hand and the Technicolor grin, he even came and gave a lecture at my school and they all loved him, even Mrs. Estabrook. Maybe he was trying to push everybody's face in it; he didn't care who knew, he didn't only want to get away with it, he wanted to be king of the world. It wasn't him that cracked open with me knowing, it was the world, and there were all the grownups standing around playing Business As Usual. Everything was going along just exactly the same, looking normal, *normal;* if it hadn't been for Tig running I would have to think I was going crazy and I'd made the whole thing up but there was Tig, still running.

So there was that sign.

There was also me. I felt dirty all the time now, there was a hundred-piece band filling my head, complete with wailers and moaners and garbage can drummers and cat gut strummers using live cats with their guts pulled out, I was the lead singer; after a while the sound got so big I couldn't hear anything else. There was something so strange about knowing, like it was my fault for being there that night and looking in his window, it was me that was to blame for seeing, for thinking such terrible things; pretty soon they were going to put me in jail for what I was thinking, I would be locked up and punished while he put on his fucking tuxedo and went off to the next dance. There were all the janitor's playing cards, face up, face up, face up, I had to make it stop.

I started spying on his house. I would go over every night after supper and try to see inside; if I could take a picture or catch him in the middle maybe I could get rid of him after all. I wanted T. Rantula to shove it in their faces, he would rip out the side of the locker room one fine morning and show the people Mr. Tilghman in the act, or crack his house open like a nut and let the truth roll out.

Usually it was just him and Mrs. Tilghman and Tig bumping around in there, you could see them through the windows of the separate rooms. They hardly ever talked; it was a lot worse than our place. Once Tig and his mother went out and I lay in their bushes in the cold until my joints ached, waiting to see if anybody was going to come to the house but nobody did. There was just Mr. Tilghman in there somewhere that I couldn't see, and me outside, too cold to keep on lying in wait for long enough. One night somebody did come, a student, and I came right up to the window and scratched my ankles getting up in the bushes so I could see in. I was holding onto the bricks with my fingers, scraping off the skin, but all I saw was the two of them talking, if Mr. Tilghman had tried anything or grabbed him I could have busted in or come back with Pop and the camera, but they just stood at the far end of the living room and talked and after a while the student went away.

I thought he might even keep some kind of a prisoner in the furnace room, when Tig and his mother were out he would go downstairs and do things, so I waited for the next Saturday when the three of them went out on some TV-commercial family shopping trip and then I went around to the cellar door where I used to get in to play with Tig. It was never locked so I went in. There was nothing in the cellar but the stuff that was always in the cellar. *The thing was spreading out of hand;* there were Tig's stuffed toys lying around, the Space Walk with its dead lights; *a bloodstain darkening the land . . .* I could feel the weight of the house on me. I looked in the laundry place and the furnace room and even that was empty: no evidence, no signs, the house and everything in it weighed about a million tons; *I still thought I could understand . . .* I went upstairs and it was creepy in their house, nobody there and everything in place. I even found the room where I saw it happening, it was Mr. Tilghman's so-called study, it had wood paneling and books with leather bindings and gold stamping that nobody ever touched, the heavy wood desk with carved

feet, and no mess at all, not even any papers in the trash;
it was fixed up the way the funeral parlor does your
corpse, so it doesn't even look used, no clues anywhere
. . . *but I was howling along* . . . something terrible happened there; the house was so heavy by that time that
I didn't know if I would ever get out from under it.
What if I wrote on the wall: I AM ON TO YOU? I
thought about breaking a window or messing on his
oriental rug, I thought all the air was going to go out of
me and I might die right there so the first time a shutter
banged I ran.

I had to keep watching the house.

If I quit watching, if I turned my back or let down for
a minute something worse would happen so I was busy
all the time now, I guess Welles knew something was up
because she kept doing stupid little extra things like
bringing books over when I didn't need them, and
dragging me back to her house after school. I would
catch her looking at me: *are you all right?* I would have
to grin and tapdance for her, yes ma'am, yesadaisy I am
fine, you betcha I'm all right, but she kept on looking at
me so hard her eyes would cross: *are you sure?*

11.

I DIDN'T WANT anybody to see me but there it was:
Pop, lurking in corners waiting to pounce, what did he
want from me? Fine, Pop, jes fine, why wouldn't a person be just fine? Mrs. Estabrook, squinting hard: was
she on to me? Welles. If Welles didn't lay off the whole
world was going to catch the scent. Not it, you guys.
But she wouldn't quit.

"Dammit to hell, leave me alone."

We were in front of school, kids bouncing on the walk
like those snake springs you get in trick stores because it
was the last day for a while, the teachers were all going
off to unheard-of places like Florida or home, they are
like the bunnies in the petting zoo, you have to let them
rest for a week so they can, ah, Go On. Welles had her

kite rolled in front of her like a silver spear and she
wouldn't budge, she just stood there with her chin out,
glaring.

"Will you lay off?"

"What?"

"Quit staring." I shook all my fingers in her face:
booga booga. "Just quit staring."

"Go to hell. Are you going to help me put this thing
together or not?"

We were like a couple of rocks in the rapids, everybody else tumbling past. I said, "I can't."

"Why not?"

"I said, I can't."

"You know what you are, Futch? You're out of it.
You've been out of it for weeks." Damn Welles, she was
doing it again, looking straight in; I guess I wasn't fast
enough. She nodded: diagnosis confirmed. "Out of it."

"Well that's just tough." I couldn't get her to back
down.

She was yelling. "Are you coming?"

Can't, I have to . . . Maybe I didn't. It was the beginning of April vacation, there would be a million kids
everywhere all week, everybody we knew and all their
friends screaming in and out of every house in the
neighborhood, the bastard wouldn't get a minute alone
so he couldn't do anything. I said, "Is that your kite?"

"My mother ordered it from San Francisco. Look at
the tail."

"It isn't so great." I let her hang for a minute. Then I
said, "You don't have any string."

"Right." She did a jumprope skip. "All right."

I didn't mind going along with her, thinking about the
kite string and not much else. I was going faster, humming along thinking it was going to be summer pretty

soon and things would be better; we started to run. Then out of the tail of my eye I caught this thing humming along beside me, going wherever I went, stopping when I stopped; I didn't have to squint or turn my head to know that it was Tig, tiny and sharp as the picture down at the wrong end of a telescope, far away but running; I couldn't get rid of it. There was always the chance I had been going at it the wrong way. If I couldn't get anything on his father or make him leave off so that Tig would stop running, maybe I still had a chance to stop it from the other end. If we could stop Tig or slow him down then maybe the other thing would be over too and everything would be all right again and if everything could be all right again maybe my mother would . . . "Oh fuck."

"What?"

"We can't do this without Tig."

"Right."

We went to get him. After we hammered on the door for a while, he finally came out. He was getting dusty-looking, like a ghost, his arms and legs looked like celery, if that's what running does for you I think everybody had better stop. I said hi and Welles said hi did he want to come out and he said he couldn't.

"Don't be an asshole," Welles said. "I've got this Mylar kite."

"I have too much to do."

"No he doesn't." Mrs. Tilghman had come up behind him and she pushed him out on the step. Right before she closed the door I looked at the eyes and I don't know what she knew or what she was thinking but I do know she wanted him to stop running just as much as I did, so there was that.

I said, "Come on."

Tig said, "You don't understand."

Welles said, "You're damn right I don't understand." She headed off without even looking to see if he would come.

I hung back. Tig was shaking like a jet on the runway right before it takes off. I didn't know if he was going to make it or not. I punched him on the arm. "If you don't come I'm going to kill you."

I didn't think he was going to but he did.

So for a week there we got Tig back. By summer he would have worked out his schedule so he could torture himself on a 24-hour basis, with exercises or research on body building or plain old running, but the April vacation had sneaked up on him and stuck him with not enough to do, there he was with all that leftover time. Even if he spent twice as long on the track in the morning he would still be almost done by the time Welles and I came along with sleep in our eyes and crumbs on our faces. All we had to do was flop on the grass and wait; he could keep on running for a while but sooner or later even he would get so tired that he couldn't keep pretending, then he would have to drag himself over and flop next to us. When he stopped gasping we would take him away and do something about it being like spring and almost summer; it was going to freeze again in another week but that week we were full of summer, running around barefoot, sticking our naked arms out to get the sun.

It was the best vacation I ever had. One day we went down into the center and spent all our money on bubble gum and gliders that broke before you flew them once. They had whitewashed the window of the local porn shop so you wouldn't know who was buying but they left slits so people could peek in. We were trying to get a look at the different plastic and rubber things when the lady came out and chased us away, she was yelling that she was going to tell our mothers and fathers on us so we went across the street where she couldn't reach us. We would howl and whistle every time we saw somebody going in; the person would try and figure out where it was coming from and when he couldn't he would get so nervous that he would go away instead. Served her right. I was ready to go home and come back with field glasses and sleeping bags but by that time we were starving and Tig had to work out on the Universal Exerciser in the gym. We told him it was really dumb; what we didn't tell him was how dumb it was because he was all pleased about this muscle he was building when any damn fool could see his arms still looked like celery, or worse.

The next day we hung out at school, it was empty and we could stand there and imagine the rest of it going on around us: kids getting trampled, ghosts of bells. When school is in we all have to be in our places by the numbers, it is all tight, which is the only reason it runs. There are all those hundreds of kids mushing in there every morning, chaos, anything could happen, murder, rape or arson, but then the bell rings and suddenly they are sorted, all going off to classrooms by the numbers: good old schedule, good old bells.

There was one classroom open and when we looked inside there was big old Mrs. Estabrook bent over like one of those bears that steals food out of the drums in national parks, she was cleaning out her desk. She looked glad to see us so we helped her cart stuff and after that she took us to a rib shop to get some takeout

food. We sat on the grass behind school and ate, feeling
good; she said when she was a little kid in North Carolina
all they ever got for lunch was biscuits and lard. At
night they would have biscuits and gravy and in the
morning they would have cold biscuits, and at noon
they would have cold biscuits, she had about ten broth-
ers and sisters and they were really poor.

I could have sat there on the grass and listened to her
all day. She had her skirt fluffed out over her big butt
like a mother chicken and she kept holding ribs and fries
and apple tarts out to Welles, to me, to Tig, and the
three of us sat there and hugged our knees and grinned
at her.

She said when she was in the ninth grade this old
farmer from down the road started coming up to their
place every night. She was the oldest so she and her
mother would have to go out on the front steps and talk
to him. Her mama used to make a big fuss over it, she
would keep making her get all fixed up after supper but
it never crossed her mind what the two of them were up
to, good Lord she was only in the ninth grade. They were
fixing to make her marry him, but as soon as he popped
the question she got scared and ran away. When she got
back she and her mama had a terrible fight and they
hardly ever spoke to each other after that but by God
she got to finish high school and after that she worked
in the dime store to pay her way to the state normal
school, by that time her little sister that was a year
younger had married the farmer with both his Cadillacs
and they already had a pile of kids. They all said she was
going to be an old maid but she was secretly engaged to
Mr. Estabrook that taught her history at college, when
they got married they left North Carolina for good.

Welles wanted to know what the moral was but she just laughed and laughed.

Tig said, "Can we come back and help tomorrow?"

She just laughed and said, "Honey, I'm on vacation tomorrow. Lord, look what time it is. Don't you people have any homes?"

I guess I knew we would end up at the river. There was this funny thing about Pop, what Pop said, about his river when he was little, the St. John's. What did I think we were going to do down there, get it all back? I didn't even know what it all was.

We bopped around all vacation like three marbles, and we ended up down there on a ricochet; there is a stretch of bank between the highway and the water, and if you can get across the road without being mashed by a semi you can slide down the bank and play like Huckleberry Finn, chewing on a blade of whatever it is that grows down there, and watching the garbage float by.

We were all on our backs in the grass, looking at clouds and not talking. I was trying to figure out what the one on the left looked like, whether you could ever paint that, whether Mom could, when Tig said, "A person could go up there to live."

Welles said, "No food."

He said, "No mess."

She said, "Nothing to do."

"I wouldn't mind."

"No people. Come on, Tig, you'd get bored."

"Well I wouldn't stay up there all the time. I could be an astronaut."

I said, "What about the group? All the money we've put into our costumes. We've got bookings, man."

Rantula, ta ta ta ta ta ta-

"You could carry on."

"The group numbers," I said, playing manager. "What about your fans?"

Welles was singing, "Show me the way to get out of this world, cause that's where everything is."

"It would be the end of T. Rantula." The group, at least, the singer: the spider was getting bigger all the time. I rolled over on my stomach so I could look at Tig. He was flat on his back with the green grass growing up around him and he was more or less fixed on the sky, so that his eyes didn't give back anything but reflected blue.

I guess he wanted to please us, he said, "I could be both."

Welles said, "T. Rantula, astronaut and great pop singer. I know what, we could all go."

"Wait a minute," I said. It was about to stop being what I thought it was. I was T. Rantula.

Tig was already running with it. "Yeah, right, we could play outer space, me up there jamming in the sky."

"Wait."

"Everybody would rocket up to catch my act."

I was hanging on to a couple of half-formed ideas: me on stage in black sequins, or tramping over the landscape, black and hairy-legged, bigger than the Astrodome, the vengeful force. "Wait a minute, who said it was going to be your act?"

"Somebody's got to be the lead singer."

"I thought we all were," Welles said quickly. "The T. Rantulas."

Tig sat up. "There is only one T. Rantula."

"Wait a minute. Who?"

"I don't know, Futch." Welles was looking at me hard: *back, damn you.* I knew what she was thinking. "Hey, Futch, who do you think should be the lead singer, huh Futch?"

You don't have to lean on me. I would give Tig any kind of present to help him get all right. "Hey, Tig, what about you?"

He was trying not to look pleased. "What do you think?"

"Fabulous," she said. "Tig's it. Right, Futch?"

"Damn right. Hey Tig, what do you think?"

"Right," Tig said, and flopped back in the grass. "Right right."

"But you would have to spend more time singing and less time running," Welles said deliberately. "You know?"

"If you're in, you're in all the way, Tig. Right?"

Tig said, "Right."

"Starting now."

"Not yet." He was so deep in the grass that I got the idea the back of him was melting into the dirt, pretty soon they would be one.

Welles said, "If we're going on the road we have to go into rehearsal."

"We don't even have all our material." I was willing to write the lyrics, if it would get him to stop running; if he would stop running I wouldn't have to keep . . . Hell if he wanted it he could be the star for life.

"Then we've got to make the demo record." Welles was getting all fired up.

I looked over at her: who were we kidding? If we hung too much crap on it, it wouldn't fly, so I said, "All we have to do is make a tape."

"Right, right, a tape."

Tig said, "We could do it on my cassette recorder."

"Great." She looked at him. "When?"

"Soon."

She was going to press him. "All right, smartass. How soon?"

He sat up again and looked at both of us with this sweet, wide-open look, admitting everything. "Just as soon as I get over my spell."

Welles said, "Oh Tig."

But he wouldn't even let us look at him any more. He got up in a hurry. "I think I hear the Good Humor man."

"On the highway? How are you going to stop him, fall in front of the truck?"

Welles said, "I don't hear anything."

I said, "It's still too early in the year."

"I heard him," he said, and it was too late to stop him.

"Wait a minute, stupid."

He was already halfway up the bank. At the top we caught up and wrestled him down; Welles had one arm and I had the other but he was stronger than we thought and he pulled us down with him so that we were rolling back down the bank in one tangle, together in the grass. We were all laughing and we dug our fingers into Tig's bony ribs so he was giggling the hardest but my hand fell on Welles and she was not bony anywhere, so I had to somersault out and Tig was next, we were both standing then with her sitting there in the grass, laughing and looking up at us.

"The Good Humor man." It was all I could think of to say.

Tig said, "Yeah, right. The Good Humor man."

Turned out he was right. The truck was still there by the time we got back up the bank and waited for a break in the traffic so we could run across the road. There he was with eighteen kids around him, backed up in the municipal parking lot. Tig bought and then he gave his to Welles and she sat on a wall and ate them both, looking at me with chocolate on her mouth that I wanted to lick off and an expression that I couldn't make any sense of right then. I pushed her off and we all just stood there, feeling good.

12.

WHEN I GOT to Welles's house the next day it was embarrassing. She was in a skirt, stockings, the works, she could hardly wait to get rid of me, and there I was in the usual, plus a grungy-looking black sweater that used to belong to Mom, with my head empty and a nothing look on my face. *I thought we were going to hang out.* Sigh. *Can't you see I can't.* It turned out later that she thought she was in love with Rich Oliver all that year, they were writing back and forth the whole time he was away at school so I guess she was already preparing her goodbyes, but I couldn't know that then. All I knew was that she was my good buddy that I had grown up with and there she was standing on their front step with this patient look, you would have thought she was explaining something to a kid.

They had to go to the Cape to help the Moons look for their summer house, they were all going to have lunch at some expensive seafood place. I could hear the rest of her family yelling from different corners of the house, Did you bring the, Comb your hair, Don't forget to lock; there she was explaining and there I was kicking her front step with my sneaker and getting mad.

"You said you would come with me and Tig."

What did I think she was going to do, change her mind? Drag me and Tig all the way to Provincetown? What were we going to do, run along behind the car or scrunch up in the trunk and breathe through the crack? Sit on the floor under their table in the restaurant? Hey, um, ah, if you people don't mind, we won't take up much room. I can get some of the dust off your shoes with my elbow here, and I will even be nice to Mr. and Mrs. Moon. Pardon me, Mrs. Welles, if you aren't going to eat the rest of that roll . . . Did I have to hold on so tight? Embarrassing but I was trying so hard to keep—something. What we had been doing all week, maybe, Tig slowing down for once and things going on more or less all right, the no responsibilities. We had been drawing a circle to keep out whatever might be coming and she had left me holding the chalk and the piece of string.

"You could stay here instead."

"I can't, Futch."

"If that's all you care about." My sneaker toe was hitting the step and bouncing, hitting again.

She sounded like my mother. "Oh Futch." Then right before she closed the door she let me know she recognized what we had been doing: she said: "Take care." She meant: *of Tig.*

"Fungoo." I threw the shopping news at their front

door and left. I went around the neighborhood for a long time because I knew I had to do it and the longer I put it off the less I wanted to. I kept thinking I would bump into Farter or somebody and they could come with me, which would take the curse off ringing Tilghman's doorbell, or else we could take off and forget Tig. I couldn't find anybody. It kept getting worse. It was like having to go and see your grandmother in the hospital, you have to do it which is why it's so bad, she could have a heart attack right there or start giving you hell because you never come to visit or even throw up on you, in addition to which you might catch it, the nurse would nab you and you'd be stuck. You have to go because you hate it, you hate it because you have to go. If I had been feeling stronger I could have holed up at home with the TV but there was this thing swimming in the soft part of my eye, the tiny picture of Tig, so there was that—that and knowing I couldn't do the day alone.

I ended up on the little rise next to his house trying to figure out how I could get him out without having to say anything to his father; if I went home and phoned he probably wouldn't come. Then they came out and got into the car. He held the door while Mrs. Tilghman got in and when he turned to go around the other side he looked up at the bushes for one minute, Dorian Gray, prettier than in the movie, did he see me? I thought he was staring right at me but then he went around to his side and got in without once changing that face so I couldn't be sure. The car went off down the street with the two of them propped up in front like Ken and Barbie and after I was sure they weren't coming back I went down and rang the bell.

He looked over my shoulder. "Where's Welles?"

"She couldn't come." I tried to look like both of us. "They had to go to the Cape."

"Oh."

He was waiting for me to say something: what? I said, "So tough."

"Yeah." He was strung in the doorway like one of those ropes when you play Haunted House; when you walk in blindfolded it will brush your face. "What do you want to do?"

"I don't know. What do you want to do?"

"We don't have to do anything." He was looking at me. He was looking at me and I got the idea he was the man in the iron mask talking to the person with the hacksaw. If I said the wrong thing he would go back to bonking his head against the wall.

"I know what." That thing swam in the soft corner of my eye; was that really Tig running or was it something else? I said, "Let's go to Harvard Square."

So we went through his mother's old purses and took off. Tig had a funny look when we got on the MBTA, like somebody escaping, and as we crossed the line into the next town he started grinning. I was feeling better too; it was like going to see your grandmother and finding out she's not sick after all. I stopped thinking about it and flashed on scenes in Harvard Square, us running into my mother, she would say, My God, it's you, and take us home with her. Then when we got off and came up onto the street I saw that practically everybody looked like her, the way she was now, that none of them were her, probably would not be her no matter how long I spent looking, there weren't going to be any recognition scenes, just me and Tig, banging around. I thought Welles and I had done something after all, because here he was smiling, miles away from the Universal Exerciser and the track.

We spent the afternoon in stores, looking through kaleidoscopes and sliding around on water beds and looking for free samples everywhere; we hung out on the streets and on the common until it started getting dark and I thought: right, time to go home and eat. I thought: Pop will be looking for me. The food stinks but at least he will be waiting under the kitchen light.

Then Tig said this weird thing. "What if we never go back?"

"I don't know what you mean." Didn't want to think about it; he would start running on me, he would run right to the river and across the top of it until the surface gave way and he sank.

That wasn't it. He was grinning, this was a game. "I mean, do you really have to go home for supper?"

"I don't know what Pop would say."

Tig said, "Mine wouldn't care."

"Neither would mine." I thought about it, Pop on the phone with her: Hello, Nina, is he with you? Why no, I thought he was with you; him calling the cops, them dragging the river, serve them right. "I guess he might."

"Yeah," Tig said, but he was looking at me, "Sure." Then he changed, maybe he was not the one who was the patient, or thought I was. Wait. "Come on, T."

"Rantula." No. I didn't know. Which one of us was the real T. Rantula? I thought it was me, that couldn't be hurt, but we had just told him he could be lead singer. What—

He was dancing in front of me. "Let's not go back."

"What's the point?"

"Just until tomorrow." His face was open, begging, "OK?"

If we didn't get back until tomorrow he wouldn't have to go out to the track to run his hundred dozen laps. I said, "I don't have any money. Where are we going to stay?"

"We can sleep at the movies." He got out his wallet. "I've got lots." We were standing right by the MBTA entrance, him jiggling up and down in his track shoes. If I said no he was going to plunge in and get on the MBTA and go right back to being what he was. He said, "OK?"

I had to do it for him. "Yeah, right, Tig. OK."

Then he did the damndest thing. I guess he wanted us to be in it together, he punched my arm and said, "We'll show the bastards, right?"

He was trying to make it into some *us* that I didn't belong to, did not want to join, who did he think he was; I had to shake him off. I just said, "Come on, we'd better go and phone."

He told his he was going to spend the night at my house and I told mine I was staying at his. Everybody said that was just fine, they were probably relieved to be without us for the night, no dumb faces at dinner, no useless questions that need answering if they are going to pretend they are doing it right, they could just let down and be themselves; I don't know what that means for Pop, tapdancing and breaking out the ginger ale because he doesn't really mind about her going, or letting the stiff upper lip go loose just for once because I am not around to mind. I will hand it to him, he wanted to be sure I had my toothbrush and a clean shirt; I said

he didn't have to worry about a thing. He didn't want
to have to worry, so he wouldn't run upstairs and check,
but it was nice of him to ask. He said Have a good time
and I said I would.

There we were in the middle of Harvard Square with it
getting dark and a whole night ahead of us, freedom, for
what it was worth. We could do anything we wanted but
there wasn't anything we really wanted to do, we had
run out of things before it even started getting dark. Not
going home was the last big thing we could think of.

When you stand in a doorway and press your hands
against the frame for long enough, you can walk away
and they will start floating up from your sides. We were
like that, floating, not really going anywhere. I thought
up having dinner, after I ate mine I finished Tig's, all he
was doing was picking at a roll. Then I had the idea that
maybe I could show him something he didn't know
about, to make up for me knowing about his father that
he didn't even know I knew. I took him to look for my
mother's house. When we found it we were going to
lurk outside and spy on them, I don't know why but I
thought it would make him feel better about things. The
trouble was, I couldn't remember what color it was, or
which one was the right street; I couldn't even find one
that looked like it, I don't know whether it was because
it was dark or because the trees were starting to come
out and everything looked different; all I know is I kept
thinking it was right around the next corner but we
would go around the next corner and it would not be
there. I thought: yeah, right, Mom. Just like you. You
have gone and moved the house.

Tig said, "Maybe we aren't going to find it."

"I'll find it."

"Maybe she's moved."

"One more block. We'll just go around one more block."

He grabbed me by the arm. "You don't have to, OK?"

The bottom half of me was still moving: one foot out. His fingers were strong. "I just have to . . ."

His voice was strong too. "I don't need to see it anyway."

I had to think of something fast or we were going to have a really embarrassing conversation. "OK," I said. "Let's go and look for whores."

By the time we got back into the square they were all out, at least I think they were. If we wanted to be sure we would probably have to go down to the Combat Zone but we didn't either of us know if we wanted to, so we just sat on a wall in an open place in Harvard Square and tried to figure out which ones were and which ones weren't, I figured fake fur was a good sign and Tig thought it was rhinestones but after a while I figured it out, I said, "It's the shoes, you can always tell by the shoes."

So for the time being I was the big expert; Tig would say, "Is that one?" and I would look and even if I didn't know I would say, "No, but that one is," or else I would let my eyes narrow and say, "Sure."

Tig got so he thought he knew and he would say, "That one, I wonder how much she gets."

Then I would have to say, "Fifty bucks," to keep the upper hand.

"You think you're so smart. What do those two charge?"

"Oh, them, they don't charge anything, Tig. They're dykes."

"The hell you say."

"I'm not kidding."

"How do you tell?"

I didn't, really, it was just a feeling, but I would have to say, "The shoes. You can always tell by the matching shoes."

I didn't know any more than he did but it was exciting sitting there because as long as we stayed there something could still happen, and even after it didn't we had spent part of one night down there where it really could.

"Did you see that?" Tig said, "I think she likes me."

"She was looking at me."

"No she wasn't, she was looking at me. You can have the other one, the one with the red candy shoes." Tig the generous.

"The hell with that, I want that one. She likes me."

"If she likes you so much why don't you go up and talk to her?"

"You do it."

"I can't, I don't have enough money."

"Well tough, I don't have any." I was glad. It might turn out we had been wrong about all of them, what if they yelled Police? What if they said, OK, men, where do you want to go? I didn't know for sure which would be scarier; I remember thinking: what the hell am I doing, I won't even be fourteen until June. Then it got really late and my ass was cold. I looked over at Tig, he was still poking me in the ribs and asking questions but his lips were turning blue. Here were the two of us with our first night of real freedom and there was too much of it. The night wasn't so much opening in front of us, offering, as yawning, waiting for us to fall in. It was too much time for us to have to fill up alone so it had stopped being a gift of anything, it was more the void.

Tig got up in a hurry. "Time to go to the show."

The good thing about the movies is, you're safe. Only a limited number of things can happen as long as there are two of you. We had to move once because of this guy but after that it was OK, we hid under the seats between shows when the usher came around to kick out freeloaders. Some time around midnight they stopped even doing that so Tig and I and a couple of winos spent the night at a French movie that since you didn't know the language you could just close your eyes and shut it out. What was hard was sleeping in the seat. I kept waking up with terrible cramps in one leg or a cracked neck, somebody on the screen would be saying, "*Toujours*," and I thought I would die if I couldn't get my legs straight, it was worse than being on a plane. They flushed us out the next morning and I felt seedy, my eyes were sandy, my mouth was all dry, my legs were pleated like Wylie Coyote's after they smash him with the rock. We went back to Brigham's, I had my pancakes and his English muffin, I was about to feel better when Tig pushed his coffee away and said:

"If we leave now I can still get in my laps."

I looked at him, thinking, Sure, Tig, sure, a whole night on a broken movie seat and brushing our teeth with wet paper towels and that's all you can think about. "Don't be stupid."

"Come on."

"I haven't even finished." I knew we could string it out if we wanted. I was about to go on and say, why don't we just: bop around, mug somebody, stand on our heads, but he was standing up.

"It's my money." His face was getting white.

"I know it's your money but you're acting like a jerk."

His jawline blurred, pretty soon the rest of him would blur too, hell, maybe he wanted to erase himself. "I thought you at least would . . ."

What did he mean I at least, what did he think I was? I could have thought up things to keep us down there for a little longer but I was getting mad at him for being stupid, for going at it that way, for . . . "It's your money."

"You can stay if you want to." He pushed a dollar at me and then he stood there for a minute gunning his motor, it didn't make that much difference to him if I came or didn't come, and I understood that if Tig was going to run I could make him put it off for a little while, maybe even a whole week, but there was no way I could get him to stop or even slow him down for long unless he, Tig, decided to stop it, so I said, "Have it your way," and we went on home.

I don't know what he did after we got there, I suppose he just went on over to the track.

13.

WHEN I GOT HOME oh my God Pop was on the kitchen phone and there was this lady sitting at the kitchen table that I didn't even know. He had his back turned and he was waving his arms and scrunching his neck on the receiver so he could wave and yell at the same time, he didn't even hear me come in.

"I don't *care* what you think I was doing, the plain fact is . . ."

"Pop."

". . . plain fact is that . . ."

"Pop, I'm home."

". . . I just can't take it any . . ."

"*I'm home.*"

". . . any longer. . . . Oh my gosh." Pop turned around

and saw me and then he covered the mouthpiece so whoever it was wouldn't hear us and said, ("Freddy, I thought you were at Tig's.") while the lady got up from the kitchen table and said, "I just came to give some papers to your father," and I looked at his face, which was changing faster than a light show and said, "Well I'm home. Who's that on the phone?"

"Yes," he said, into the phone. "I'm listening. Of course I'm listening to you."

"I'm Helen Chandler," the lady at the table said, shuffling a mess of papers and fanning them so I could see all the dittoing and Xeroxing and handwriting: business, see?

"Oh." I had a look that Welles said would kill rats; I tried it.

I guess it worked. "Helen Chandler from the history department." She pushed the papers around. "History papers, see?"

("This is Helen Chandler, Freddy, Ms. Chandler and I are team-teaching a course next semester.") Pop uncovered the mouthpiece and got back to whoever it was on the phone. "I am listening, I've said everything I can think of, I don't know what else to say."

Maybe I stuck my finger in the toaster by mistake, I was buzzing like something you've just plugged in. "Is that Mom?"

He was saying, "I've paid until I'm tired of paying. Don't you think enough is enough?"

He and Mom never fought about money. "Who are you talking to?" But if that wasn't Mom, why was his face squashing like a mashed paper cup? "Pop, who's that on the phone?"

This Helen Chandler or whoever she was was sweeping

all the papers up out of the crumbs on our kitchen table and stuffing them into her briefcase. "I have class in another ten minutes so I'd better be . . ."

"Please don't say things like that."

". . . going."

"If that's Mom I want to talk to her."

("Thanks for everything, Helen. We'll get together on that next week. Freddy, will you shut *up?*") He started talking back into the phone without taking his hand off the mouthpiece; when he noticed it he got all flustered and started over. "No, nothing. Just Freddy and his little friends."

"What friends? Is that Mom?"

"It's school vacation week."

"I said, *is that Mom?*"

"Goodbye, Ted."

("Goodbye, Helen. I'll call you on that. Oh Nina, please don't.") The receiver was trying to jump out of his hands. "Oh Nina, please don't, I can't talk about it now, I don't want to talk about it any more . . ."

"HEY, MOM? HELLO, MOM."

("Stop that. I can't hear myself . . .) Spare me the comparisons and I mean it." Why couldn't he get a decent grip on the phone? Sweaty palms, butter on the receiver or what? "Oh God." Then damn if he didn't hold out the phone to me; anything to change the subject, anything to get her off. "Fred has something he wants to say to you."

Nobody does that to me, nobody. "I do not," I said, and backed out of reach.

"Fred, it's your mother."

Not it, Pop.

"I'm your *father*."

I backed off to where there was no way he could reach me without letting go of the phone. "Well big deal."

"What? What's that?" He had faced up to it and was sighing into the phone. "He was right here a minute ago but when I turned around to put him on he just disappeared. Yes, I'll tell him you're dying to talk to him. Yes, I know he'll be sorry too."

I was thinking: If she wants to talk to me she can come home and talk to me. "I am not."

"Yes, I'll tell him." He could hardly wait to get her off. "And I'm sure he does too."

"The hell I . . ."

"And you know how I feel." He swallowed his voice, I don't know if she heard that, I don't even know if she heard him say goodbye.

When he hung up I said, "Who was *that?*"

"That was your mother, Fred. Now don't be facetious."

"No, I mean with the briefcase."

He was very busy splitting an English muffin. "Oh, that. That was just Helen Chandler from the history department."

"Well who is she?"

"Somebody I'm teaching with, that's all."

"She got butter on all her stupid papers."

"It's just a spare-time thing." He had the muffin in the toaster, he could hardly wait for it to come up. "You grab all the meetings you can get." He was hanging over the toaster and when the muffin wouldn't come up and wouldn't come up he stuck in a fork. He put the two halves on two pieces of paper towel and put butter and honey on them. Then he pushed stuff out of the

way on the kitchen table and made me sit down with
him and take half. He wanted to know did I have a good
time at the Tilghmans' and I said yes; if he hadn't been
out of his mind with everything he would have been
able to figure out that I wouldn't be caught dead at
Tilghmans', but what did he know? He didn't want to
ask me too much and I didn't want to ask him too much
so we just sat there and ate English muffins until the
whole pack was gone and I would have to say it was a
good idea because while it was going on I could just sink
into it—good old home, good old kitchen, good old Pop.

Right, it was complicated: what we were doing. Some
girl wrote in Pop's yearbook in the old days and I found
it when I was going through some stuff in the attic. *It's
not what you're doing, it's what you think you're doing
that makes the difference.* What we were doing was getting through. Pop's way was making with the English
muffins and the class schedule and things at the office,
as long as people could see him doing what he always
did, he could be OK. Which is why he got up before I
was ready and started collecting his stuff.

"Where are you going? I just got home."

"*Alice in Wonderland.* It starts at two."

"But that was something of Mom's." She got him into
it right before she split.

He just kept on putting things in shopping bags: the
bunny ears she had made for him, some fuzzy bedroom
slippers, white socks to put over his hands. "That's no
reason to bug out."

"She did."

He was rummaging in the kitchen drawer where she
used to throw old lipsticks. "There are a lot of things
wrong with me, but I don't back down."

"What does she care? She won't even come."

"I care." He shoved one of the shopping bags at me, holding it out until I had to take it. "All right?"

"All right."

So I helped him carry his stuff over to the football field where the rest of the Drama Club was flapping around behind the bleachers getting it together while the chamber music group sawed away in front. The whole thing was kind of confused because they had never gotten everybody in one place to practice; somebody had written this verse play and now they were handing out mimeographed copies and the director was running around with a megaphone, getting everybody into place. I went around front and lay in the grass on the hill and watched. It was wonderful. All the costumes were in Playskool colors, there were giant playing cards and banners and right after it started somebody let loose about a thousand helium-filled balloons. It didn't matter that nobody knew their lines because the orchestra was playing and the wind took the rest of it away. The looking glass was turned so the sun flashed in everybody's eyes and we never did get to see the caterpillar because Arnie Moon's father had slipped a disc, but it was OK because everything looked so, what, *pretty*, partly because it was a nice day and partly because we all wanted it to: them, doing it, and me, watching. The Red Queen and the White Queen even looked pretty, Danny's Girl Scout cookie mother and Patty's mother, looking like somebody out of some other fairy tale, with little girls in party dresses and crowns of flowers carrying their trains. The girl ushers were pretty and Farter's father's girlfriend was pretty for once, with her hair down and a blue Alice dress and a pinafore that covered up everything that was going on underneath. Everybody looked fine and springy and hopeful, even Pop in his borrowed fur coat, sweating and laughing with the rest of them, dancing in the new grass. In case you were losing track they served pink lemonade during the Mad Tea Party, there were students running around barefoot carrying trays while everybody that was left over put on giant playing cards made out of posterboard and ran around squirting red food coloring on things. It was silly, right, but it was nice. It was nice sitting out there in the sun even though there were more cold days coming and it was nice just seeing them all dressed up and laughing, being nice. Everybody was smiling and flapping around, you could see they loved being all dressed up and acting silly, it didn't matter what they went home to after or what the insides of their heads looked like because right now everything was as good as it ought to be. Even I was nice for once, lying there in the grass and watching them carry on, you could see they were tickled to death because the audience laughed no matter what they did and it made everybody feel so good, the ones that were doing it and the rest of us. I thought: *all right*. Welles came over and sat down without saying anything and toward the end Tig came in from running and flopped next to us so we were all three of us there in the grass with the music playing and the mirror flashing and the colored balloons going up and everything was so pretty that I got the idea that maybe this was what you had to do. If you could bust your ass making things nice maybe you could get people to be the way they should.

14.

POP SAID she was my mother and I had to go.

I said I didn't want to.

He said he was worried about her.

I said, "Bullshit, you don't even care."

We both knew that wasn't true but I wanted to bring him out in the open. His jaw was working; if he hit me then I would know for sure, but he wouldn't, not him, not Pop, he was being, listen carefully, adult. That is not what we grownups do here in the last quarter of the twentieth century, we are fucking civilized. He hauled back with one hand and then his jaw let go; I thought, the eyes are next, they are going to bloop out and roll down his face.

I wanted him to hit me.

Instead he gave me a sermon about holding on to things by letting go.

There was nothing to do but walk out on that one so I took my flight bag and I went, right, I had already packed, I did it as soon as she called and asked me to come because I really did miss the hell out of her. I didn't get mad until I realized what they were making out of all this: the ritual weekend with the mother; next stop: the divorce.

Pop followed me in the car all the way to the MBTA. He kept calling out of the window, trying to give me a ride. I kept saying no thanks. Why should I? It was only three blocks.

So there I was back in Harvard Square but at least she was waiting for me so I was spared that one, and I was also spared trying to think up the right thing to say because we just hugged: her boobs, the ponk. I thought, oh God Mom, what makes us have to go through all this? Then we had to let go because there was somebody else there forcing his hand at me and I was supposed to shake it, this beanpole with a beard, Fonda type with watery eyes. Mom was breathing in and in until I thought she was going to pop, I was thinking: *is this all?* I thought he would be big bear, big stud, big something but all he was was . . . Mom said, "This is Al."

All I could think to say was "Oh."

"Al. It's his community. He's the head of the house."

He kept on sticking out his hand. "Pleased to meet you, son."

When I didn't do anything or say anything Mom pulled somebody else around for me to be polite to, old lady she must have been fifty, but in jeans and running shoes the same color as mine; her face was all pushed in:

not heavyweight fighter, pug dog instead. "And this is Angel. She and I are writing the play."

She knew I wasn't about to shake hands so she didn't even try. She just looked at me, I might as well have been somebody out of the funnies, your life-sized cutout Charlie Brown. "Al, he looks just like Nina. Nina, he looks just like you."

"I do not."

"Improved model, I hope." Mom was grinning and flapping, if I wasn't careful she was going to get hysterical and take off, like Snoopy fluttering his feet. "I guess he's a little nervous."

"I'm not nervous."

"We're all a little nervous."

"Not me."

"I mean, this is a lot all at once." She couldn't stand another minute of it but she couldn't figure out what to do.

"He'll be all right. Right, Fred?" Al clapped a hand on my shoulder: the warden, the kind that tries to motivate. "He just needs time to get used to us."

I would like to find time to blow him up. I was scowling at him. I knew whose fault it was.

Mom pretended to be taking my pack, she was whispering, "Are you all right?"

I said, "I'll carry it."

"We'll get Fred here an ice cream and then look into that coffee house I told you about." He took off before I could tell him I didn't want any, and Mom, Mom just trotted behind without even looking to see if I would come.

Angel said, "A coffee house is going to be too big, Al. This is a small play."

Mom said, "We can try it out at home. If it carries, it will carry anywhere."

They went on talking so I didn't have to; Mom dropped back and tried to hold my hand like when I was little but instead we walked along bumping, you know, hey; by that time we were knocking elbows because she had started getting short. When we got to the house I had to look in all the downstairs rooms, Gerda or somebody had made the curtains, Al had built the sofa, she, Mom, was doing a painting for this room here. The only other time I had seen her like this was when they stuck some of her paintings up in the Faculty Club; she was pink and shy and proud. She introduced me to Ella the junk sculptor in the basement and somebody named Arthur was writing an endless novel upstairs, he showed me the stack and said he was already up to page 2,943. Then it turned out Al had clients waiting in the office and he had to go.

Later on I would go in there and read some of his books about doing it, I couldn't figure out why people needed books on doing it when I could go crazy just looking at the books. I thought Mom was going to take me up and show me the bed where they did it every day and every night and after breakfast but instead he was dragging her into his office and I was stuck out in the hall with old Angel, that didn't like me any better than I liked her.

She said, "Well." She couldn't figure out what to do with me or her hands either, she kept running one of them up the bottom of her face, not wiping that smile off her face: trying to wipe one on. "Uh, your mother has to work now. She has to help Al."

I didn't say anything.

"She's really good with his patients."

I still couldn't think of anything to say.

"I mean, she can talk out of her own heartbreak, you know?"

"What?" That was my mother she was talking about, my *mother* that was in there telling people how to run their lives, it made her sound like somebody I didn't even know.

She gave up. "I could show you the rest of the house."

"Don't bother."

"You want to watch TV?"

"No thanks."

She was getting mad at me. "Don't you have any hobbies?"

"Not really."

She kept wiping the smile on and wiping it on but she couldn't get it to stick. "When Al's kids come they work in the garden."

"He has kids?"

"His wife keeps them."

"He's *married?*"

"Isn't everybody?" She was scowling, daring me to say I didn't believe it. "Even I was married once."

"Oh."

"Will you stop staring at me?"

"I'm not staring. I was just."

"I was married and I had to lick his loafers clean in the morning and lick the toast crumbs off his face and that's not all I had to lick." She was getting madder and madder. "I mean to tell you, it was shit."

She was waiting for me to say something. I covered my mouth and went wmp. She could take it any way she liked.

"Your mother is a nice pretty lady. She doesn't need that kind of shit."

I was swallowing hard but I would die before I would let any of my thoughts come up to the top.

She was really mad now—at me? At what? "Do you know what I'm talking about?"

"Yes Ma'am."

She was yelling. "Call me Angel."

"Yes Ma'am."

"Well do you want to see her room or not?" I don't know why but she was about to kill me, she was going to punch me out if she had to spend another minute with me so I said that would be OK and she took me up to Mom's room and shoved me in and shut the door.

It wasn't anything like I thought. The first shock was that she had a snapshot of Pop and me stuck in the mirror over the dresser and the other one was that there was a studio couch that was only one person wide so whatever she and Al were doing I guess they had to do it somewhere else. Somebody had set up a cot for me over in one corner behind a screen so I threw my stuff on it and began to spook around. She was on the pill, which I guess I had more or less known before she left us but never really thought about, and I counted how many were left and read all the warnings, etc. they had printed on the pack. She wasn't washing her clothes too much and I could tell she wasn't painting because the brushes stuck in the coffee can were crusty and stiff. I knew she wasn't finishing anything because I found a couple of crumpled-up letters to my father, there wasn't enough on the paper for me to make any sense of it, and I had a pretty good idea she wasn't finishing the play because there were pages and pages of messy handwriting, probably Angel's, and only a couple of scraps by her, typed notes with a lot of crossing out, and this one crazy poem that I stole after I read it because for the first time I had the idea that maybe she wasn't hanging out down here just to make us feel bad or even because she wanted to do something really stupid, what she thought was, she was on the edge of something ready to jump off, like a bird with its wings stretched out.

I was going to be the mother of us all
and I only had the one.
I was going to be the beloved
then, well—
I was going to be the painter/writer/nerve physiologist
anything but the bored and boring
left over
and left out,
I wanted everything, why was it wrong for me to want
   all that?
Was I the only woman/girl ever to want all those things
   or did everybody else get it
except me?
I am the husk, all that is left of the mother and provider,
   did he do this to me or did I,
I don't even know who is to blame.

   Then there was, oh Mom:

Why couldn't I be the golden girl in the silver gown size
   four
with the hips like coatracks and a Ph.D. in linguistics,
belly like a saucer

with silver words dropping from my honeyed lips
Is it the more you want the less you get or have I got it
  wrong and it's the other way,
Is it the less you want the more you get or is there not
  enough getting for my wants?

Then she came in and all I could think of to say to her
was, "If you take the pill you're going to die, it says so
on the package."

She just hugged me and said, "Oh Freddy, you don't
know what you're talking about."

What did we do after that? She asked me a lot of questions about Pop that I didn't want to answer: Was he
eating enough? Did he seem all right? Then she got in
two months' worth of questions about my teeth and my
hair and my homework, wedging them all in at once,
and after that it was time for dinner so we went down.
Everybody worked. Some of them were crashing around
in the kitchen and other ones were setting places and
bringing up the chairs, Mom brought in the milk pitcher
and we all sat down, Al at the head, everybody else
along the sides. I recognized Angel and Arthur with the
endless novel, he came in with his notebook and wrote
down everything that was on the table and then came
around and got every one of us to say something so he
could put that in. There were about ten others that I
never did get their names, guys and some I guess they
were still girls, a lot younger than Mom, they would say
Al this and Al that and I could hear Mom next to me
tuning up, it was like living in the Trapp Family Singers
or Show and Tell or something worse. Al kept trying to
impress me, he was saying fuck and shit a lot to show he

was just one of the guys and not uptight like Pop, he put his hand on Mom's hand halfway through dessert and after a while I had to spill my milk.

He wouldn't quit even after dinner, he was fanning out and having a word with this one and then that one, bopping them on the head with his magic wand like the Great White Fairy, I think he was getting off on being the most important person in that house, everybody was hanging around and grinning: me, Al. Me. Me. He even did one on me, about how Mom was, ah, Working It Through, I didn't want to stay around and watch her wait for her turn so I went upstairs. When I looked over the rail she was hanging around like a lost Girl Scout that the troop had left for somewhere else without her, and I thought: she left us for this? I spooked around alone in her room for a long time, chewing it over.

So yeah, I was lying awake when she came up to bed, I lay there on the cot behind the screen wondering how long it would take before Al came in, whether they would check to be sure I was asleep. I thought I would wait until they were in the middle and then maybe I would take the lamp and smash him. I didn't hear him at all: just her slipping out of the Indian shirt and into whatever she wore to bed, going to the basin in the corner to brush her teeth. Then I thought maybe she would cry herself to sleep and that would be something, when we got up in the morning I could say, Mom, I'm going to take you home. She didn't cry. She only sighed a couple of times and got in bed.

It was getting light when he came in, I don't know how much I had slept or what I had imagined; I don't know where he had been all that time or what he had been waiting for but there was his voice in the room: Nina. I could hear him rustling. She took a while to wake up and I held my breath; I hung on to the edges of the cot like an astronaut waiting for the blastoff: here goes, but I didn't know where. After a while she woke up and recognized him. "Oh."

He kept his voice low but I could hear. "Did you forget?"

She rustled. "I'm sorry, Al."

"Well, did you?"

Her voice was low too, tired. "No, I didn't forget."

"Don't you know it's almost morning?" I guess he was pulling on her. "Nina?"

"Al, I can't."

"What's the matter?"

"Fred." Fred what? I had my ears, eyes, mouth, everything open trying to hear better.

"He won't even know you're gone." He was about to stop whispering.

"I just can't."

"Nina, I don't wait."

She sounded like she had cotton in her throat. "Don't you think I know that?"

"Nina?"

She just rolled over, I could hear her flopping, I guess she turned her face to the wall because he slammed the door going out. She waited a long time, maybe to see if the slam had waked me; then I heard her cry. I wanted to get up and offer to beat him to death for her, but I knew better. I just waited and after a while she stopped and a while after that she went to sleep. It was getting light in the room and I couldn't stand just lying there so

I pulled the covers off with my toes, inch by inch, and then I sneaked into my clothes and let myself out and went downstairs.

His office door was open but the files were locked, so all I got to look at was the books. He had all those books on doing it, which is not as simple as you might think, plus a lot of stuff about weird children, so I sat there and read until I heard people getting up. There was somebody rattling in the kitchen; I went out and there was Angel making eggs. It was too early to talk so she just gave me some and we sat and ate. After a while Mom came tearing in, she had combed her hair with her fingers and she looked a wreck, I guess she was afraid I had run away or something worse: His Bed Hasn't Been Slept In. When she saw me she said "Freddy, oh Fred," and grabbed me around the neck, squashing my face because she was still standing up and I was sitting down. I thought, I don't think I can stand this for a whole weekend, our nerves, and I guess she was thinking some of the same things because she said, "This isn't much fun for you."

"It's OK."

"I guess your father will be missing you."

I thought about him soloing in the house. "He might."

She said, "You can see I have plenty of people here."

"Yeah?"

"I'm going to be all right."

I just looked at her, so she had to say:

"Are you?"

"Who, me? I'm fine."

When I didn't say anything more she had to go on. "I thought maybe we would look at this sculptor's studio and then have lunch and I'll send you back, OK?"

"That will be fine."

She was trying to get me to look at her. "Freddy, do you want milk or coffee?"

"Either will be fine."

"Look," she said. "Your father."

"He's fine."

"What. Ah, what are you going to tell him about me?"

So I looked at her. "What do you want me to say?"

She was thinking hard, I could see her face changing for every thought that went on behind it, if we'd had time she might have gotten it together to tell me, but by that time we weren't alone. He was standing behind me but I know who had come in because of the way Mom's face changed. The way she looked I thought he and the other woman must have come in together with their hair wrapped around each other's faces, but when I turned and looked it was just old Al. In another minute Mom was going to forget what we had been talking about; before she did she said, fast, "You can tell him I said hi."

"I'll tell him you're fine."

I liked the sculptor's place; she was making the entire city of Boston out of junk she had found, the parts she had already done were like being inside a funnybook, she had a Big Pru that you could go up in and a Big Cock that looked like one. We got to help her make foam-rubber ladies, sewing foam rubber around the arm bones and stuffing newspapers in the front of the Thrift Shop clothes. I thought I would like to move into that city of Boston where everything was funny and off scale but everybody was more or less smiling and none of the people could talk back; they stayed where you put them, which is all a person could ask.

Afterward we took our hot dogs over to the park and

she tied herself in knots trying to explain. I guess all that, what she was saying, was her trying to figure it out. She wanted to give me something to take home after all, something to tell Pop so we would both lay off, but the more she talked the worse it bothered me and the worse it bothered me the harder it was for her to quit or me to let her quit so she just kept babbling long after she wanted to be finished because we couldn't either of us let it go.

She said, "The thing is, when you fall in love you disappear into a person, and then if the person . . ."

What? "If the person what?"

She went on as if I hadn't asked. "Pretty soon there's nothing left of you." She said, "I was invisible. I would wake up in the morning and if he wasn't there I couldn't go out because I wasn't anybody when I went out alone: not him, not me. After a while I couldn't even go to the store any more. When people stop looking at you, you disappear."

T. Rantula was unfolding inside of me, black hairs snagging in soft places, one elbow at a time. Back, damn you, back. "If the person what, Mom?"

This time she heard; she got this funny look but she was not about to answer. She said, "I have to find out who I am."

"I know who you are." She did not want me to answer you are Nina Crandall you are my mother, maybe there was nothing she wanted to hear from me but I could not stop pushing, had to push. "Mom?"

She stuck her chin out and put up her hands to stop me talking. "I have to find out what I want."

"If you're trying to explain you're not really explaining."

She said, "I wanted to tell him about this letter I got,

from Ellen, that I knew in college? She had both breasts off and everything out and now it's in her brain so she's going to die in a couple of months but she thinks she has it figured out, what everything is *for*; I had to tell Ted the day I got the letter, there I was by the door with tears in my mouth and he came in and didn't even see me, he just kissed me and went right to the phone." She took me by the shoulders. "I had to do it, Fred."

T. Rantula was talking back: get that woman away from me. "That isn't any reason."

"It was like dying living there."

"Mom!"

"I did it for all of us." She was begging me to buy the package. "Fred?"

"I don't think those are very good reasons."

Her fingers bit my shoulders and she surprised the hell out of me, she flashed: "If that isn't the real reason I don't want to talk about it."

I was waiting for her to come out with it: *I don't love you.* Go on, get it over with. "Mom?"

She said, "I don't know what I'm going to do."

What was I supposed to say?

She wouldn't let go of me. "Don't you see?"

The change was going faster than I thought; if I didn't get her to let go she was going to see T. Rantula in another minute, he would grab her in our jaws and lug her back to our house or else savage her right here, I had to get away before the change was complete, I was going to have to get out of her sight. *I don't love you.* If I could just get her to say it, something straight, that I could understand, and fight . . .

She said, "It's not that I don't love you, it's something else. Something you can never understand."

I started prying at her fingers.

"But try." She was waiting for me to say I would, repeating, "Try to understand," she wouldn't let me go until I said I did, or at least nodded, I would be trapped there forever with her explaining without making sense, going on and on right up until the minute that she looked into my eyes and saw the real T. Rantula; I closed my eyes and squashed him down for the time being so I could nod and get her to let go. If I had been Pop down there on the bench with her maybe I could have done it better, said the right thing, apologized if that was what it was, been strong enough to take her home, but it was only me, Futch, swallowing the other thing, so I sort of mumbled, she could make what she wanted out of it, at least it sounded friendly, and she mumbled back. Then I just sat there and she just sat there waiting for me to finish my hot dog that I hadn't even wanted and then she hugged me and said she guessed it was time to put me on the MBTA. At the end I ducked my head so she wouldn't have to see my face.

On the MBTA he got out for good and ranged the car with hairy legs rattling the windows with every step he took, an eight-beat pace that got faster and faster, not the trapped creature pacing, just the monster thinking, knowing it was time to put an end to it and trying to figure out how, by the time I got out at our town center I thought I knew so I went over to the college and hung around outside the English department, from where I was I could see his office window and the light was on; I don't know how I had known he was going to be in there but I knew. I had the shakes, I was getting cold from the fingers and toes all the way in to the center and I was scared I would stop breathing, I was scared to death of passing out but I hung on because I couldn't stand it any longer, I had to get to him and stop him if I could. By the time he came out I was spastic, jerking up and down in the grass until I could hardly get moving, but I finally managed to rattle over to where I was standing on the walk where he would have to push me out of the way to get past, I was shaking so hard I could hardly stay in one place long enough to find the words and get them out.

"Mr. Tilghman." I guess he didn't even hear me the first time, my voice was so faint.

He just kept going.

I ran and got in front of him so he would have to stop. "Mr. Tilghman, I know what you're doing."

Well he looked at me without even seeing. "Oh, Freddy, it's you."

I was getting dizzy, I didn't know if I still had enough breath in me to make a noise, I finally managed to find some and with the last strength I had I forced it out: "I know what you're doing and you'd better stop."

Then he brushed me aside without even looking, I could have been a gnat or a bead of sweat rolling down his cheek except he never sweated, I wasn't any more than that to him; all my suffering and planning and spying and figuring had come to nothing because he just pushed me out of his path and said, "Oh Freddy, go away."

15.

WHEN I GOT HOME Pop had all his crap out on the dining room table, he was doing the breast stroke through the eight hundred thousand index cards he has collected for this book he hasn't been able to finish ever since I was little. Even though I was going to throw up if I wasn't careful I had to stop and talk to him because he was so thrilled to have something else to do, he could play Pop and stop having to think about *that* for a while: what he was supposed to be doing and could not do. Then he got a good look at me and decided I was sick.

So he put me right to bed and I decided to let him. It was a relief to be lying there in my room letting the shakes work themselves out through my fingertips and

looking at my dumb posters and my dumb, empty gold-
fish bowl that I forgot to clean it and they died and
dried out in with the rocks; it was a relief not having to
think and not having to do anything about anything.
Then Pop came up with some soup and crackers on a
tray along with a dish of ice cream, invalid food, and sat
by the bed and talked to me for about an hour. Partly
he wanted to know everything about Mom and the
house down in Cambridge and everything in it, did I
really think Al was an OK person, was she all right, was
she all *right,* but partly he was there because he thought
I was really sick and he wanted to be nice. Maybe I was
sick. I was laid out flat and I didn't care whether I sat
up or not. As long as I didn't try to, I wouldn't have to
find out for sure.

Pop ate half my soup and gave me some of his beer
and I told him all the things it was all right to talk about,
building the city of Boston and listening to Arthur read
parts of his endless novel, when Arthur writes about a
house he has to put down everything it's made of and all
the things that are in it including the kind and number
of the nails and the history of every single person and
every single stick of furniture because Arthur truly
thinks that everything is part of everything else and as
long as he can keep from getting to the end of what he
is doing he isn't going to have to settle anything, like
how it's going to come out. I told Pop about Al's books
on doing it and Al's office with the bust of Freud and
the big teakwood desk and I left out how Mom was
helping with the patients but he got mad anyway. I
knew I had better not tell him any of the things she had
tried to tell me to tell him and I didn't show him the
poem either; I was remembering Al in the night, what he

had said to Mom when she wouldn't go with him, but I couldn't tell Pop about it because he would get the idea that she had left for one reason only, to get at him, and not really because of Al, which is what he wanted to believe. As long as he could blame it on Al he wouldn't have to look at the rest of it.

The whole time we talked he was shaking his head. I said Angel was a tough mean lady and I didn't really know about her, I didn't like her much and I knew she didn't like me. Oh tich. Arthur had this problem with reality, which is why he started the novel. Tich tich. According to Al's notes one of the main problems with married people is they don't want to know the truth. He sort of groaned,

"Oh no."

"I had a pretty good time."

"I never should have let you go."

"No really."

"Look at you, it's made you sick."

"I'm not sick."

He was looking at me hard. "I suppose you think it was something you ate."

I didn't want to think about Mr. Tilghman. "Maybe it was the stew."

"Poor kid."

"What the hell do you mean, poor kid?"

"This isn't any kind of childhood."

That made me mad. "I'm in the eighth *grade*."

"You should be out on the river, or playing with your friends."

"You mean like Tig?"

"All your friends," Pop said. "You shouldn't have to . . ." His face was changing, he had found something that was going to make him feel better, he had decided to do something about me whether I wanted it or not. "I'm going to take you down there and show you what it's like."

"Huh?"

"The river. Everything." He must have been running movies behind his eyes. "The one thing they can't take away from me. What about it, shall we go to Florida?"

"*Florida.*"

"The St. John's River, you could sit on our front porch and it was like being on a ship." He was building something in his head. "I need to get away from here so I can think. It'll be good for both of us."

"You mean just bug out?" I was thinking about Mr. Tilghman, all that responsibility.

"I'll get you excused from school. You'll only miss a couple of weeks." He looked so helpless. "How does that sound?"

I would do anything to get away from the responsibility. "If you say so. OK, Pop."

As a result I missed the eighth grade dance, I missed graduation night which was no big deal, anybody who has lived around a college knows you really only graduate once and it is not in powder blue gowns when you are barely fourteen, but I was sorry about the not going down to Brigham's with all the kids afterward, I got the idea school was never really over because I didn't get to throw my notebooks and papers on the fire or go back with the other guys at midnight and piss on the cornerstone. I missed the class picnic and getting my yearbook signed, they had to send it to me in the mail; in fact I missed most of last summer, it just left without me.

What I did not miss was watching Mr. Tilghman; it was

a damn relief, we were so far away from there that there was no way I could watch him and by the time we got back he was gone. So I stopped watching him and maybe that's the reason it happened the way it did but maybe it would have happened anyway; when we got back Tig was already in Mass. General which I did not find out until September, because Welles was in England with her family so there was nobody around to ask. Half the world was in summer school and the other half had gone to camp or off to visit relatives so I was going to spend what was left of July and August reading and drinking ice water, all because Pop had the idea that his past was better than my present and he had dragged me down there so he could try and pull it out of the swamp grass and hand it to me, he was like Jennifer Jones in that movie about the Catholic saint, scrounging around in the mud trying to pull out something wonderful with his naked hands.

There isn't much to tell about the trip, it was all six-lane highways and Holiday Inns, one place looked like every other place and you could always have the same thing for dinner no matter where you got off. The only difference was the land got flat and sandy as we went along, the trees pooped out and there were these scrunty-looking pines and a lot of brown grass. As soon as we crossed the Georgia line Pop started to jangle and by the time we got there he was hopping out of his skin; I thought that was wild since we were supposed to be on vacation, and it took me a while to figure it out.

That's only a curtain, Pop.

Your sheets are not attacking you.

For Pete's sake, even I know that's the ice thumping down in the ice machine.

His eyes were getting blacker and rounder. I would say hello and he would say EEEEEk.

When we got to Jacksonville Pop found us a two-room apartment over a garage with one of those cabinets that folds out to make a kitchen, the paint was peeling and there were roaches. I slept on the couch and Pop got the bedroom because he had to have room for the big mess of papers and boxes of books we had lugged in and out of every motel between there and home, the story he put out back at the college was that it was now or never, this was a voyage of discovery, he was going to break the back of that damn book. Now he has been working on this book all my life and you would think anything you had been writing about for that long would get finished, but the piles looked just about the same to me when we stuffed them back in the car a month later, except he had woven another color of ink into that patchwork quilt he called a manuscript; I thought if it was now or never and it turned out not to be now, the smart thing would be to chunk it in the garbage when we left, there would be more room in the car for my feet, but no, not Pop. Besides, the real reason we were down there was the river. When he was a kid Pop lived in a house right on the banks of the St. John's River down in Jacksonville, Florida, and whatever it was like then, that he remembered, we were going down there to get it back.

The funny thing was we didn't get out on the river for a couple of weeks. I had the idea Pop thought it would be too heavy to go down there right away, everything was heavy for him now that we were away from all the usual stuff: what you did at certain times of day. He had been OK since Mom left, he was in better shape than me and I remember being pissed off at him: Buddy, don't you even care? It turned out the only thing holding him up was the routine. Without it he just crashed. It wasn't bad compared to what Farter's mother did, or the biology professor who broke every pane of glass in the college greenhouse and tried to cut his wrists, but it wasn't too good either. The shying at window curtains was only an early sign. I didn't figure it out until one night when I got up to go to the bathroom, there was Pop in the bedroom with the light on and all his junk spread around him on the table, index cards, dozens of books, papers with so many colored lines they looked like the insides of a telephone, zillions of words that he just couldn't get together, I could almost see them sliding around under his hands. I went in and peed and went back to bed and when I got up in the morning he was sitting in the exact same place, he hadn't even moved his arm. He couldn't fix it and he couldn't quit. I hit him on the arm and said, "Pop?"

At first he didn't even notice me. Then when I jerked his elbow he spread his hands, trying to touch all of it at once.

"I can't." He looked scared and it scared me.

"Pop, do you want to come and eat?"

"Can't. I have to."

I remembered Tig: No you don't. I said, "I thought you said you can't."

"Go away and let me think."

"Do you want me to make some eggs?" He was, like, paddling around in the middle of all those papers, he was either going to sink or else he would float over the falls with Mom already up the creek, pretty soon there would be only me and I would be stuck in that dump forever, he hadn't even taught me how to drive. I wanted to burn the book or blow it up, I wanted to take every one of his stupid books and papers and index cards and different colors of ink and all his ideas that he couldn't get together that it made him feel so guilty and put them in a garbage can and roll it off a cliff but I couldn't do that, I couldn't do any of it. What I did was, I punched him hard on the arm, I was screaming: "Have it your way. Starve to death."

So he had to look at me.

I was still yelling. "I'm going to make some coffee and you can either have some or you can go to hell."

Then I guess he saw me. I was shaking all over and all my hairs were standing up. "Freddy, what's the matter?"

"Nothing!"

"Easy." He was trying to hold me down.

"Do you want the fucking coffee?"

"Coffee." He wanted me to get calm so he got calm. "That sounds fine. Make some french toast while you're at it, I'll be right along."

So I made breakfast and we ate it together, he went back to work but he quit right away when I called him for lunch and washed his face before he came to the table. We were, what, keeping it together for each other. Around three I said let's *do* something so we went out in the car. After we got the routine set up it was pretty much OK, if one of us started sliding the other one would say, Oh, hey, time for X, whatever it was, and we would get on with the routine.

When we were driving Pop had trouble finding things, his old school and where his friends used to live, he had moved away when he was fourteen. He couldn't exactly get us out on the river because he didn't know which was the best place to rent the boat, I think he wanted to string it out because once we did that there would be no more reasons to stick around. Driving used up the afternoons and by the time we fixed dinner and cleaned up after, we were home free, we could sit up on the sofa like kids getting over the chicken pox and watch TV. We had to sneak up on his old house but we finally got there, at least I think we did. We worked up to it, starting with what used to be the dime movie, and the corner store.

Pop said, "You could get it all for a quarter right there on that corner. A dime for a funnybook and nine cents for the movie, you got candy with the rest."

"Yeah, right." I was looking at those crazy sidewalks, made of the eight-sided pieces with weeds growing through the cracks.

"A quarter."

"Neat." Every time I ask for my allowance he does a number on how broke we are. All I want is money to buy those same things.

"I never wanted you to have a better childhood than I did, or even the same one. I just didn't want it to turn out so sad."

"It's OK, Pop." What was he trying to get back for us?

"Oh Fred."

The next day we went down to where he thought the house was, there were creepy black trees with grey stuff hanging off of them. Pop was staring into all the houses, I got the idea he wasn't sure which one it was. Finally we stopped.

If that was his old house, it was a wreck. All the houses on the street were old and saggy, but this was the worst. It hadn't been painted for longer than the other houses hadn't been painted, there was stuff growing over everything and the yard was full of junk, your rusted tricycle, your ice box with the door ripped off. If that was it, was he ever happy there?

"Is that your old *house?*" He used to make it sound like the next best thing to a Mississippi riverboat.

"I guess that's it."

"Gee, Pop." It was terrible.

"I guess it doesn't look like much." He was scratching his head and he couldn't get the parts of his face to match. "They kind of let things go."

I couldn't stop looking at him looking at it. It had taken him three days to find his old school and he hadn't found his best friend's house at all, or his best friend, either, he got me all the way down here and here was this terrible-looking old house that he wasn't even sure it was it. "Maybe we should look at the river instead."

"The dock is probably rotted away." He didn't try to get out of the car. Instead he turned and took me by the shoulders. "It didn't used to look like this."

"It's OK, Pop."

"It was right after the war, we had to take what we could get."

"I said it was OK."

"Watch your tone."

Pop wasn't getting out of the car but he wouldn't leave either, it was getting late and we might starve to death right there, I was thinking about us bronzed or petrified, still sitting there with our butts spreading a hundred years from now, all ready for the archaeologists, so I said, right in his ear, and loud, "Are you getting out or not?"

So he started to, he was halfway across the dirt when
the lady with the dogs came out of the house next door
and no she did not blink at him and say, Why, aren't
you little Teddy Crandall, that used to live around here,
and he didn't get to say, Why yes, and she did not have
us in to make his memories come true with a lot of talk.
All she did was threaten to turn loose the dogs, and
when he said he used to live there she said the hell you
say, she was either young enough that they used to
play together or she was old enough to remember his
mother, she was ugly as hell in that flowered dress and
she knew it, she said he had better clear off right away
or else. It was embarrassing. All right, he didn't stand up
to her because he is this terrible gentleman, but he
wouldn't let go either. He got back in the car all right
and she went back in the house but then he just sat
there.

"I'm sure if we could get around front you would see
it."

"Well we can't."

"I wanted to show you the river."

"There are lots of other places."

"Not the same."

"Who cares?"

"I care."

I thought about the trip, that rotten apartment, all
those hundreds of dozens of hours of bad food and
dumb TV. "Well I don't give a shit."

"I wanted to show you the river from here."

Everything about him was thin. His hair was thin, his
face was thin, even his mouth looked thin but all I could
think of how I was feeling, all those dumb motels, all
that stupid sitting in the car. I tried to make the key

turn in the ignition. "What the hell difference does it make?"

He knocked my hand away and more or less automatically started the motor. "Oh hell, Freddy, I don't know."

It turned out the next day we got out on the river after all, Pop had stacked all his index cards and put them in boxes before I ever got up, by the time I finished eating he had even made a lunch for us to take, along with a six-pack and too many Twinkies, he has this idea he can make things up to me if he just lays on enough food.

We rented a rowboat from the fat old guy in the state park and we piddled around through the channels in the sawgrass, there were places where I could stand up and it would still be taller than my head. We took turns rowing until Pop said, "There."

The water wasn't too great, it didn't look any better than our river at home, it even had some of the same stuff floating in it, but it smelled different, salty, and the sky was different—different light, different birds, different-looking clouds. If you did it right, staying in the channels and looking mostly up, you could pretend it was back in the old days, when Pop was a kid. I got thinking it probably had been a lot different, he would have been able to row clear out in the middle without being swamped by a garbage scow, maybe none of the factories were there back then and it was jungly-looking instead. There were gulls, looking whiter than any I had ever seen, the sun was white and I could hear stuff crackling in the sawgrass, giant bugs or baby crabs. Pop didn't say anything when I took a beer so I drank it and lay back in the bow, thinking maybe the whole trip had been worth it after all. Maybe we could just stay out here on the river, Pop would quit the college and buy a houseboat and we would never have to go back. Mom could go to hell.

I said, "You could go out to sea if you wanted to."

"Not exactly."

"Did you ever row as far as the center of town?"

"We were only little kids, Fred. The currents were too strong."

"I thought you said you could go for miles."

"It only seemed like miles."

I wasn't paying too much attention, I was just lying back with the sun on my eyelids, breathing in the salt muck. Lying there, I could be anybody, and finally I said, "Now I see what you mean."

But Pop was remembering. "There was always a lot of noise from the air base, planes going in and out. Once there was a crash in the river and the water was full of blood, chunks were washing up for days."

I was watching the action on the inside of my lids; it looked like a lot of neon sperm. "What if we never went back? We could live down here and she could go to hell."

"Freddy, I never really belonged here."

"But your friends."

"They weren't really my friends."

So his memories weren't true after all and I had to sit up and look at him, I blinked and squinted and looked at him sitting there in the sun with the sawgrass rising behind him, there we were out on his river that he had never stopped talking about and there he was, this pale, skinny guy that looked like he didn't even want to be out in the boat. With my eyes open I could see how hot it was, waves of heat like jelly in the air, and there were about eight thousand bugs in our boat alone. "Yeah," I said. The whole thing was just another of his cons, but I didn't know which one of us he thought he was fooling—what we needed this for. "Right. Sure."

He wasn't listening, he wasn't even looking at me, he was seeing something else. "Did you know your mother used to come around to my place in Cambridge and throw rocks at my window? It didn't matter what I was doing, she knew she could get me to come down."

"Oh. Her." My brains were boiling. I think it was a hundred and two.

"You should have seen her then, with shadows on her cheeks and her hair blowing in her mouth."

Something was biting and I itched all over. "Let's go, Pop."

"We were like a couple of wires crossing, I could feel her all along my bones."

The neon sperm were swarming, they were bursting in my face. I said, slowly, "It wasn't great and you know it." She said so.

He said, "It was too great."

"And this isn't great either. I hate it down here." I was thinking about Al, the poncho, the ponk. "Let's go, all right? Let's go back in there and go home."

He said, "I would have jumped in the Charles for her, I would have done anything, and she . . ."

"You're making it up, just like all your stupid memories."

"Now she won't even talk to me."

"She won't what?" Right, maybe she wouldn't, but I didn't know that. Which one was I wrong about? Neither? Both? In another minute Pop was going to turn to me like he thought I had the answer and ask that

same old stupid question: *What went wrong?* The top of
my head was coming off.

"Fred, what's the matter?"

Right, I did what is never done, I stood up in the
boat: when I told him about Tig's father he had tried to
pretend there wasn't anything the matter, maybe he
thought it would go away. Maybe he thought this was
going to go away. I couldn't stand it, I was straddling
the seats, I was mad as hell without knowing why, that
was me lunging at my father, wanting to hurt. "If you
loved her so fucking much why did you let her go?"

And then my God he said, "Because I don't have any
right to keep her."

I fell onto my seat. "You—don't—what?"

"It's my fault," Pop said, and drooped so his knuckles
were dragging in the bilge.

"Oh shut up."

"What I did, what Annie and I did, oh Freddy I didn't
want to have to tell you, I guess Nina didn't either, but
sometimes a marriage just gets to a certain point . . ."

I didn't want to hear it. "Shut up."

"So I was the one."

"Well you can go to hell." I was up again, I didn't
want to hear. What was I going to do, push him out of
the boat?

But he was into it, confession, he wasn't going to let a
little thing like me stop him, he was strangling on it,
coughing it up, "It was me that was unfaithful first."

So she had told me all those things that didn't make
any sense and none of them were true, and he had let
me believe whatever floated to the top, both of them because they didn't really care what came out of their
mouths, had kept me from the truth or the truth from

me and now he was trying to force it on me so in the end nothing was true or right and I couldn't stand it, could not stand thinking about it; I was on my feet and moving, yelling, God damn, and I don't know if I was leaping for his throat or what but I was flying and I guess I missed him because I was in the water, I jumped or fell out of the boat. I could hear him yelling from behind me, "Freddy, what are you trying to do?" I probably could have headed for shore and been able to stand up in another minute but by that time I was flailing out toward the middle of the river, maybe I thought one of those big boats would come along and suck me up into the screws.

"Freddy, come back."

I just kept on swimming.

"This is crazy."

"Bastard."

Stupid bastard, he was just standing in the boat and yelling, "Freddy, that's *enough*," and I didn't even look at him I just kept going and he just kept yelling, "Freddy, you don't even know where you're going," until finally I heard a splash and he was swimming after me. I thought I was fast but he caught up before I could even think about getting away from him and he was mad as hell, he grabbed my foot and yanked me back where he could reach me and then he pushed me under, I dragged him down and spun around as we came up and hit him in the face, I hit him and he hit back and we were both choking and hitting, I don't remember what we were yelling but I know I wanted to kill him and I think he wanted to kill me, but the water kept getting in the way, slowing every swing either of us made, so we ended up wet and sobbing so hard we had to stop swing-

ing and start wrestling and pretty soon instead of
wrestling we were hugging, coughing up water and I
guess laughing until suddenly Pop let go and backed off.

We just glared at each other, spitting and treading
water, and Pop looked right into me and said, "You're
pretty bad off, aren't you?"

"Fuck you, I'm fine."

Then he said, so quietly that I had to strain my ears
and open up my mouth wide to help myself hear him:
"All right, Fred, I'll take you home."

"You mean off the river?"

"I mean home."

Then he turned around without looking back to see if
I was going to follow and struck out for the boat and I
was too tired to do anything but head after him, one
water animal following the other water animal, going on
instinct, I guess.

So we went back off the river, we checked in the boat
and got some of our money back for the time we didn't
use, it was so hot our clothes had already dried so Pop
took me to a junk food place in a three-mile mall for a
Blimpy and a batch of french fries, my native food. He
was already beginning to talk about leaving for home; I
was slupping up the bottom of my milkshake when he
rattled his throat and began to, I don't know, apologize,
not *for* anything, exactly, except, ah, maybe not being
all there, he knew it was hard, and so I had to look at
him and say I was, um, sorry for yelling and he said he
guessed we were both upset and I said probably that was
it. Then he said, "People don't always end up doing
what they thought they were doing when they started
out to do it." He had his hand on my shoulder, I guess
he was feeling better because he thought he had made

me feel better, and I was feeling better because I had let him, when you know somebody is watching you are more careful about your act. After that we went to the movies, another Clint Eastwood, with so much blood and guts that it was just a lot of pretty colors. The sweat dried out of my clothes and I could feel my muscles seizing up from the air conditioning but I didn't care, the seat was good and we were alone in the dark except for a couple of kids that came in late and sat down with their legs over the back of the front row; I threw my legs over the seat in front of me, thinking, *Yeah, my place, and these are my kind of people.*

Afterward we got groceries: Yodels, Ring Dings, Jiffy-Pop, salted everything, and went out to the car. The air was still hot even though it was getting dark; there was a lot of racket from the highway and the air was mostly food smells and exhaust. We stood there for a couple of minutes in the middle of all that neon, asphalt, shopping center, Muzak, McDonald's, your commercial usual, our country, ours.

Then Pop said, "I hate what they have done to Florida."

This is the world, Pop. You might as well live in it.

Not Pop. He had to blame something. He spread his two hands to hold it. "All this shlock."

My country. I said, "Oh Pop, why did you wreck our family?"

He just looked at me and said, "Be quiet, Freddy, you don't know anything."

We got into the car and then we sat there, him too tired to start the motor, both of us gentle and sad. "I know we're here."

Kids," he said. "You're the last damn moralists in

America. Kids only know part of it, all you know is black and white . . ."

"I know when something's *wrong*."

He went on as if I hadn't even spoken. ". . . you just sit and look at us and judge."

16.

WHEN I GOT BACK everybody was gone. I got a post-
card from the Tower of London which I couldn't read
because Welles always writes her postcards standing up.
Tig was off somewhere; his folks were on Nantucket,
which was a relief, but later on I found out Tig wasn't
with them. First I heard he was at camp and then the
story was that he was at his uncle's farm getting over
mono and then it turned out he had been in Mass. General all along, but nobody would say which part until
September when Welles and I went over there to find
out and his mother cried. It turned out Farter's father
had gotten married over the summer, he and the fairy
princess were going to have this baby so Farter had to
go live with his mother in Minnesota and we would only

get to see him at Christmas; who knows, another time it could just as well be me. I read and drank ice water. I started to write a movie about a rock singer in the Foreign Legion, nobody knew he was anything special until the regiment got in danger and they discovered he had this powerful thorax and the silky black hair growing down his arms onto the backs of his hands . . . Also I painted my bedroom black, even the ceiling, I figured what the hell.

In August Pop and I went down to Cambridge to see Mom's play, it was in a storefront and they gave us wine in paper cups and passed the hat afterward. Maybe Mom thought Pop was good for twenty bucks and that's why she invited us; I don't even know why he wanted to go. He was writing on his book, don't ask, he was also going out with Helen Chandler that was so charming you wanted to punch her in the mouth. I don't know who Annie was, that he said he did it with, but she didn't come around. Mom was waiting for us on the corner by the Coop, looking like somebody escaping from Russia with all their clothes on their back. I guess she had borrowed one thing from everybody in the house. She had those skirts that you have to wear at least three and shirts with the tails out and the belt wasn't enough, she had to have chains, she was all elbows and jewelry. I don't know how she did it but her hair was different, it was not exactly Afro, more like the lady's after they plug her in and turn her on in *The Bride of Frankenstein*. I don't know if she did it to impress Pop or give him the finger or both, but she looked so weird I was kind of proud of her: *I am no longer one of you. See my powerful thorax and the black hairs growing down the backs of my hands.*

They were both nervous as hell. She said hello to him
and he said hello back and they were knocking themselves out not showing anything, but then Mom hugged
me and she held on so tight that we were all three of us
embarrassed, it was like I was the only thing she had left
to hug; she smelled different, and when Pop asked her
how things were and she said wonderful, I thought it
was a lie.

He took us to dinner first, there we were in this expensive restaurant with him looking square and her like
early Halloween, and all they could think of to talk
about was the food. Pop had the runs I guess, party
flutters, he kept going off to the bathroom so when he
was at the table we would all eat and mumble the same
things again, they were tugging on either side of me and
I got the idea they were scared to death I would try to
go off to the bathroom and leave the two of them sitting there. Every time Pop got up Mom and I would
talk.

"Helen Chandler," she said.

"Yeah, I hate her guts."

"Is he—ah—serious?"

I looked at her hard. "What difference does it make?"

"It doesn't really matter," she said, fast. "I was just
wondering."

"If you want to know these things, you should stick
around."

Then dammit to hell she said, "Sometimes you can
stick around and not know those things."

"You never told me about that part."

"There are some things we shouldn't any of us have to
know."

By that time he was back among us and we did an

insane number on the weather that got us through the meat and salad, and he took off again while we were waiting for dessert.

"Do you think he misses me?"

"How am I supposed to know?" I was unwrapping soda crackers and stuffing them in my water glass, it was the kind of thing that used to drive her crazy. "What about stupid Al?"

"I'm not with Al any more," she said. "It's someone else."

"Well who?" I fooled around with the mush in my glass and shuffled through the rest of them that lived there, who it might be, but she wasn't answering, so I had to say, "I said, who?"

"That was never the point."

"I don't see why."

Damn her she said, "You wouldn't understand," and started telling me about the show. Then she said, "Does Helen ever sleep over?"

"For God's sake." Cute, Mom, knock it off, Mom. I stuffed another cracker into the mush, thinking I wished it was her and Al or Arthur or whoever it was. Whatever Pop did, he didn't want me to have to think about it, which was more than I could say for her. I went on with the crackers; partly the glass was so full and ugly it was getting interesting, partly I was thinking that if I let it slop over it would get on her nerves. After a while she would have to say, "Will you *stop* that?" so we could be mother and kid again; friends was more than we could handle.

Instead she just kept at it. "I was just wondering . . ."

I could see him coming out of the men's room and by that time I was so mad I said, "He said everybody's got to get it somewhere."

"Oh Freddy!"

She was so hurt that I was sorry right away and I had to lean across the table and whisper to her, partly to tell her and partly so he would see the two of us being close, because she needed it. "He doesn't even like her, I don't think."

There he was again and we had to think up conversation. We couldn't do the weather again and we had already ordered dessert, I had said yes I was excited about going to high school in September, so I had done my part; we had talked about the play a little and now it was Pop's turn. He said, "Fred and I went down to Jacksonville."

She had been keeping track of us. "I heard."

"Remember the time you and I went out on the river?"

She melted and oozed all over the table. "It was like something out of the movies."

That was before I was born so I just let them play all their old tapes while I ate dessert; at last they had found something they wanted to talk about and I thought except for Mom's lady playwright costume and the mush in my water glass we could have been anyone, Average American Family out for a night on the town. I wasn't listening to all the words but the tune sounded OK so I felt it was safe to leave them long enough to go to the bathroom. They didn't even look up when I came back.

When Pop got up to pay I asked her why she didn't just come home with us after the play. All her layers of clothes started flapping at once and she got busy stuffing them back; no matter what she pushed back in something else popped out, and when she finally looked at me her face was just as disorganized as the rest. "Oh Fred, it's not as simple as you think."

While she was off in the ladies' room sorting her layers out and fishing beads up from her front I said why the hell didn't he just drag her home with us in spite of everything.

His jaw squared off like Dick Tracy's. "That's not the way life works."

We were just about nose to nose, which was interesting because I used to come up to his shoulder. "Why don't you punch her up and make her come?"

"I want her to be happy, Fred."

"Who says happy is the big thing?" I was trying to figure out what else was important: keeping it together. People's feelings. Me.

He was looking sort of crazed, I thought he was going to push me into the coat rack. "Who the hell do you think you are?"

But there was Mom hoving down on us so I just slid out from under. "I guess we'd better hurry, right?"

She looked like the Queen of Sheba in all that jewelry and she scooped me up without even looking at me. "Right."

When we got outside I hung back because I didn't want to walk with them just then, the black hairs were pushing out through my shirtsleeves and dripping off the backs of my hands, the bad thing was they were not the ugly ones, I was the one, but if I was the one I didn't understand it, would never. There was one thing I did understand after that night, the most important. I am always going to say what I mean.

The play was just Mom and Angel acting out a lot of Mom-and-Pop fights with a couple of songs, one funny one, about food, that Mom wrote, and Angel, ralphing: up against the wall.

Her song went:

> Chain of suffering the death
>   death of soul
>   death of body
> There is nothing but death when we come together,
> all our children are wrenched out of blood . . .

I liked Mom's better. They wound up with a couple more songs and a softshoe: "This is the end, this is the end . . ." About halfway through Mom realized she was singing alone and she looked over at Angel, who was fishing this piece of paper out of her front, I guess Mom was doing her best to try and head it off because she started dancing hard and singing louder: "This is the end of our show . . ." if she could just finish and get off fast, maybe she could take Angel with her. Angel wasn't budging, she pushed Mom out of the way and started hollering:

> No more from us you bastards
> No more meals stretching into oblivion
> We will not bloody our legs to bear your children
> Any more. Smear your faces with our blood and cry . . .

Poor Mom, she gave it one more try, dancing like a puppet on speed and yelling the finale:

> We hope you liked
> We hoped you'd like
> We hope to like
> Our show . . .

so they were both dancing with Angel bellowing:

Fall on yourselves for your sex and solace for we are free
And we will kill to keep it that way . . .

after which she flopped her head down so all her hair
fell forward and there was Mom pulling on her, poking
and hissing until finally she picked up the song and they
finished the number together. By that time Angel got
interested in what her feet were doing and they kicked
offstage, the lights went out and everybody started
clapping because they were so relieved.

When they came back out for a curtain call there was
hardly anybody left but Pop and me and, this was nice,
most of the people from the house, everybody else had
escaped. I saw Arthur and them, no Al, still clapping. I
thought we ought to go over but Pop was stuck to his
chair. He said, "Which one's Al?"

"He isn't here." I stopped watching Mom for a minute
even though Angel was breathing hard and talking fast
and they were about to give Mom the flowers. Pop had
his fingers clamped on the edge of the table, was he mad
at the play or at her? I thought: maybe now he will do
something.

"Where is he?"

"I don't know."

"You must know something."

"Besides, I don't think it's Al any more."

"You what?"

"Nothing." They were all up there with her, Arthur
and Angel and the junk sculptor and all the ones whose
names I never knew, if she wasn't with Al she might be
with somebody whose name I didn't even know, but

who? They were all hugging and swaying, trying to make her feel good and I don't know whether I wanted to bomb in there and blow them apart or just have a chance to be part of it for once. I said, "Aren't you going to congratulate her?"

"I thought it sucked."

"Then why don't you tell her?" One way or the other it would be something; Pop wasn't helping at all, he was seeing whatever it is Pop sees and when I got up, trying to get him to say whether we were going to stay or go, he didn't even see me. I didn't have to think about what to do because Arthur came over and got me so I knew it wasn't him. Everybody was saying Hey Freddy, Hi, even Angel was being nice, she stuck her whiskers into my face and growled, "Is that the rat bastard over there?" and without even thinking I growled back that it was. Arthur had his notebook with him and when I looked over his shoulder he was putting me into his novel, what I had on, what I said, so I got to be in the middle after all.

They had started closing the place and Mom's friends were piling outside to wait for their ride. They pulled her hand but she said wait a minute and went over to speak to Pop. I stood around by the bar, pretending to be somebody else, because I didn't want to have to hear what they were going to say, if they were telling lies to each other there was no point me listening and if they were telling the truth I didn't want to have to hear. She might ask how he liked the play and that would start it off or he would say: Who is he, and I didn't want to hear, but there was no way for me not to because they were yelling.

"Not good enough for you, Nina, it's not *up* to you: none of it, none of them . . ."

"You don't have any idea what is and is not up to me. You don't even know who I am."

"I know who you are, and you're not that play."

"That's my best, and if you don't like the best I have . . ."

"Forget it."

"It's what I am now, and the sooner you realize it the better."

"Hey, Nina." There was Angel standing in the doorway.

"You're mine is what you are." I don't even know if he believed what he was saying.

"Nina, our ride's here."

She looked cross and confused. "In a *minute*." There was somebody else standing outside, when she saw who it was she moved around to block Pop's view.

"Who's that?"

"Nobody."

"Is that Al?"

"What difference would it make?"

"I could talk to him."

"I suppose I could talk to Helen Chandler."

He jerked back in two stop frames. "I never told you about . . ."

"Or Annie Rand."

"How did you . . ." ·

"Freddy told me. So now I guess we're even."

"If you want to look at it that way."

"Maybe that will make things easier."

"Nina, who is that out there?"

"Nobody you know." There was Al in the doorway, hitching his thumb over his shoulder. Come on, come *on*. She just gave him a little wave. But if they weren't even doing it, why should she, and who . . .

"If that's Al I'll kill him." Pop's voice was lifting: there, that's something, at least.

She sighed. "Go ahead, it won't make any difference."

There was Angel. "Your ride's leaving."

"In a *minute*."

"You mean if I did you wouldn't come back anyway?"

"That's not what it's about. Ted, I have to go."

"Nina, please stay with us."

Her voice was low. "You know I can't."

"Please think about it."

At least she didn't say no. I had been pretending not to look because it was so embarrassing but when I did they were both standing, she was pulling away from him so she could go out and get in the bus with Al and the rest, but at the last minute I saw her fingers dragging across his wrist into his palm and he was saying, fast, "Are you happy?"

She was halfway out the door by that time and she kept on going but she turned for a second, whirling so fast that all her bracelets rattled, and for a minute I thought her hair was on fire, she was flashing: "That's not the point."

17.

COLLEGE OPENED UP, the light changed and we were into September. Pop's classes started on Labor Day, I guess it was what he had been waiting for because he was off down the middle of the sidewalk, zap, he had quit jumping every time the phone rang and he was even sleeping in the middle of their bed by then, he had left off leaving room for Mom. So there was all that to keep him going: classes, meetings, freshmen sitting on the floor outside his office, waiting their turn. Which left me. In olden times I spent that week on line at the doctor's and the dentist, I would be getting new track shoes and jeans and stuff, including school supplies that I would never use but liked the color of: plastic notebook dividers, the six-color ballpoint, the cheapo Day-Glo ruler, but that was Mom who used to take me around and cough up money like a gum machine and she was down in Cambridge with Al or was it Arthur, she wasn't going to catch the back-to-school ads in *Up Against the Wall* or whatever it was she was reading, *Screw*, or *Psychology Today*. So I started high school with some desk stuff I ripped off from Pop's office, his shirt fit as long as I kept the sleeves rolled up and I hated breaking in new track shoes anyway, mine were exploding and they looked just right. The place was so huge I didn't find anybody I knew, Welles wasn't getting back from England until Wednesday and when I called to find out if Tig was back from wherever he went over the summer, all his mother would say was he wasn't quite ready to start school. Farter and Rich Oliver were gone for good and Patty Westover had been sent away someplace where they could keep an eye on her. Even the Tuccis were in a different section, so there I was with three thousand strange people that I was mostly shorter than, knowing only that invisible was best and you didn't go into the bathrooms, ever; I didn't put in all that time at the Hiram T. Chandler Middle School just to start all over at the bottom.

Welles came over as soon as she got home. I got off the bus and when I got to the house she was on the front steps, no hello, all she said was, "I can't find Tig."

"When did you get back?"

"Just now. I heard he wasn't at school. He isn't anywhere. What happened?"

"I don't know, I haven't seen him."

"Why not?"

"I just didn't."

She was standing out on our front steps in her old jeans and black T-shirt with a new haircut from England, I guess, looking better than I had ever seen her, and she

didn't even ask how was I, what was new, all she wanted
to do was complain. "You mean you didn't even go and
look for him?"

"Get off my back."

She had her thumbs hooked in her belt loops and she
was rocking on her toes like Welles; later I would find
out she had been around all summer with this English
guy that was almost eighteen, she had probably been
doing a lot of things, but there she was grinning like
Welles, like we were such good buddies that I would
never, ever get to do any of those things to her that I
started wanting the minute I saw her. The body wasn't
new but this year it was softer around the knees and
elbows, hard to explain, I could not stop looking but
we were good buddies and I knew she didn't want me
to look. "All right for you, Futch."

"All right, I didn't go and look for him." There was a
thing about her jeans, the way the legs met at the crotch.

But she was looking at me head on; with me at least
she wanted to be, what, Just One of the Guys, and I was
supposed to let her. "Well, why didn't you?"

"For God's sake Welles, they just got back last week
and besides." I wanted to forget Tig and hold her.

"Last week? They've been home a week?"

"I thought he would call." Back, down, go away.

"They've been home a week and you didn't do anything?"

"I've been busy, all right?" Remember, this is Welles,
and you can never. We could still hang around together;
I already knew it was going to be less and less, we would
probably be able to talk about almost everything, but
never everything. Not ever again.

"You could have gone over."

"I thought he was still at camp or something. He was

supposed to be at his uncle's and besides." I was scared of being reminded. Had put away several things when Pop and I took off for Florida.

"You should have checked. He could be sick or something. He was so weird right before the summer."

"Well I couldn't go over there."

Then she backed off. "Hey, are you all right?"

"Why shouldn't I be all right?" I was getting mad at her. "Why shouldn't I be fine?"

"Then let's go."

"No, you."

"Both of us." She was giving me the *High Noon* look, trying to dope it out. "Futch?"

"Wait." Why was I scared to look into his face?

"Unless there's something the matter with you."

"Up yours." So she had faked me out.

Which is how I ended up back under the artificial gas lanterns on their doorstep, I imagined there was red gunk from the lava lamp still stuck between the tiles. Nobody answered at first and I was dancing backward off the porch, I was going to be behind Welles in case the door opened and if it didn't I would be the first one back in the street, if we got going fast enough and it opened at the last minute I could pretend not to notice it. Who did I think I was scared of, Mr. Tilghman that didn't even notice me? I was scared to see Tig.

I said, "Nobody home, let's go."

Welles just stood there with one hip out, ringing the bell and chewing gum.

Finally somebody came, I could see her shape through the curtains in the little window on the door. When she stuck her head out she didn't even say hello how were we, she just said, "He isn't here."

So I was spared that one, having to look him in the

face knowing I forgot. I was carrying all that stuff for both of us, thought I could find a way to get rid of it, and then I just—forgot. "OK Mrs. Tilghman, bye."

Welles snagged my elbow with one finger. "Wait. Are you sure he isn't here?"

Somebody had drawn lines on her paperdoll face. "I said he wasn't, Eleanor."

"Then when will he be back?"

"For God's sake, Welles."

She didn't even hear me. "Is he coming back today?"

"I told you, he's not here."

"We could wait." She was trying to push the door closed on us but Welles was leaning on the handle, pushing back. "Mrs. Tilghman, what's the matter?"

"Matter? Nothing's the matter." She was stranger than I had ever seen her, her paperdoll face was cracking, sad to see.

"Then where is he?" That was me asking because Tig was not here after all and there was nothing left to be afraid of. She wanted to get that door closed so bad that we just had to keep it open.

"I told you, he isn't here right now."

"If you'll tell us when he's coming back then we can come over when he gets back."

She gave up pushing on her side of the door and looked at us both straight for the first time. "Not for a while."

"Is he sick?" Damn Welles, she should have been a private eye.

"Sick?" Mrs. Tilghman looked confused for a minute. "Where did you hear that? He's fine, just fine."

"Then why can't we see him?"

"Well he's having a little extra . . . well, it's an extended vacation."

When she gets like that, Welles won't let go even if you beat her with a stick. "We'd really like to see him, Mrs. Tilghman. When did you say he would be back?"

Mrs. Tilghman was all over the place by that time, fluttering around in the doorway and looking so messed up that I had mercy and tried to get Welles to quit. I pulled on the back of her T-shirt. Out. Come on, let's get out.

Not her, not Welles. "But school's already started and he's missing a lot of work."

"Oh, that. Well . . . he may be going to another school. As a matter of fact he might be going away to school, maybe even Andover." She could see Welles was just about to nail her so she said, fast, "It won't be for a while because he's, uh, he's away right now, he's having a little rest."

Welles said, "There."

So by that time she was ready to cry and she told us that Tig was in Mass. General but she never did say what for, maybe she thought if she told us we would go away. At the end Welles thanked her and apologized but we had to find out because he was our friend and Mrs. Tilghman said she understood; maybe she did. Then Welles said she would like the address so she could send some candy, which was a lie, and we found out which unit he was in. That was when Mrs. Tilghman finally cried, which I don't want to see ever again. One minute she was looking like the perfect fashion person on her way out to roll in the autumn leaves for the photographer and the next she was wrecking her hair because she thought if she could just run her fingers through it enough times she would be able to stop crying, which she couldn't, the tears just kept on going down into the lines around her mouth. She didn't want us to go see

him but we wouldn't promise. We just said we hoped he
would get better soon, if she wanted we could get the
teachers to send him assignments so he wouldn't get
behind. Welles said, I'm very sorry, Mrs. Tilghman, but
we had to know, and she nodded and even smiled because she almost had her face back together and she
thanked us for being such good friends.

"There," Welles said, as soon as we got away from the
house. "I told you. Something's wrong."

I just nodded; maybe I already knew.

"So I'll pick you up at ten on Saturday. Think about
what to bring him."

"Wait a minute."

"We have to go see him."

"Wait." I don't know if I can.

"I'm not going by myself."

"Mass. *General.*"

She had cut her eyes at me, showing whites. "Unless
you're the one that's sick."

I fell for it. "There's nothing the matter with me."

"Then I'll pick you up at ten."

So she had faked me out again.

Saturday we took some copies of *Dude* and *Playboy*
along with a book of Escher prints that Tig had always
wanted and went down to Mass. General. Sure I was
scared. I didn't know what was the matter with Tig. I
knew what was the matter with me: I had forgotten. All
I had to do was that one thing and keep doing it, watching him, and I had forgotten the minute Pop and I
crossed the Massachusetts state line, that's how long I
had lasted. Whatever it was with Tig might not have
happened if I had been able to keep my mind on it, it
was such a stupid little thing and I had let it go for the
simple selfish reason that I wanted to.

So there was all that piling up, the guilt, plus not knowing what he was going to look like or how he would be. I thought he might be plugged into machines and not even know us or shrinking around in one of those white things that fly open in the back, or they might have to pry him off the wall so we could speak to him; I didn't know what to think. The surprise was that it was OK; except for the fact that he couldn't move too fast, it was really pretty much OK. When we got to his floor he was dressed and out on the hall, it could have been Tig on any other day except there was a big wrinkle of jeans in back where he had taken in his belt and his shoulders were sticking out like coat-hangers in his T. Rantula shirt, which had been black like mine and Welles's, but had been washed so many times that it wasn't any color in particular. Like Tig, when he finally turned around. The other thing was there was a nurse walking with him, together they were pushing along this chrome tree with a couple of bottles hanging from it: I.V., you could see tubes going to taped places in his arm. They were laughing and talking and Tig didn't even see us until we got close enough to hear them: he was explaining that he had to get off the I.V. soon so he could go back to running and she said where did he expect to do that and he swung his hand around in this grand sweep that I remembered from a lot of other conversations, and said she would have to clear the halls. Then he heard Welles hem-hemming from behind and turned around so fast that he almost tore the needles out of his arm.

We looked at each other hard while the nurse fussed with the tapes and needles, getting it all back in place. He was no color at all and his hand was shaking so hard the nurse could hardly tape the back of it, I thought:

what if he doesn't want us to see him looking so terrible
and weak but he wasn't even embarrassed, he just
grinned.

Then Tig said, "What kept you?"

Welles was flashing the *Playboy* where the nurse
wouldn't see.

Then I said: "T."

And Tig said: "Rantula."

So we knew everything was going to be all right.

By that time the nurse had the second needle taped
back where it belonged and she said to Tig, "Ralph,
you know you aren't allowed to have visitors."

He said, "God, Futch, Welles, you're not supposed to
be here."

Welles said, "I just got back from *England*."

The nurse was saying, "I'm sorry, but he . . ."

I said, "Why not, are you catching?"

Tig said, "No, it's blackmail. I don't get to see anybody I like until I eat."

"Except of course his parents."

Welles said, "My mother sent some cookies." She had,
too. I could see the grease coming through the box.

Tig started to say, "You don't . . ."

"Wait." The nurse was thinking fast. "Maybe I can . . ."

". . . understand," Tig was finishing, but by that time
the nurse had headed off to consult with somebody at
the desk.

When she came back she looked important and excited. Maybe she thought we would, as they say in the
trade, Do Him Some Good, she might have thought we
were the miracle cure, we might even wedge some of
those cookies between his teeth, we would keep pushing
the crumbs back in and make him swallow. She said she

had gotten special permission for us to stay till four and then she got very busy moving us all into Tig's room, him and the I.V. rack and me and Welles and the magazines and the cookies, which was hard because there was almost as much junk in there as he had at home. He had a TV and a portable stereo and a CB rig and a typewriter and all the books and magazines and plastic toys that the lovable old Tilghmans could lug in there instead of having to stay and talk to him, a load a day for longer than you would care to think. Welles and I had to take stuff off chairs to make a place and there was barely room on the bed for Tig, the nurse had to brush aside eight hundred things and together they got him in, it took a while because he was really weak.

"All right," Welles said after the nurse left him and he got his breath back. "What's the matter with you?"

"Anorexia." He was looking, I don't know, vain: *I told you I was sick*. "Anorexia nervosa. You know."

Welles said, "Like hell. Only girls get that."

He looked so proud. "That's all you know."

"Oh. Oh wow." I was trying to sound impressed because that was what he wanted but I couldn't quit trying to figure how much I had to do with it, what if I had started earlier and kept my mind on it: his trouble, what I should have done.

Welles was getting impatient. "Well when are you going to get over it?"

"You don't just get over anorexia."

She said, "That's so *stupid*."

Tig flashed. "What the hell do you know?"

"But you can get over it any time you want to." She kept on top of him. "All you have to do is eat."

Tig moved his hands up, the left one carefully, so he

wouldn't yank at the needles. He was hugging his shoulders. "It's not as simple as you think."

"I don't see why not. All you have to do is have one of these cookies and it's over." Welles pushed the box at him.

"No thank you."

When he wouldn't take one she tried to hand it to him. "Go ahead." She was ready to push it at him, grind it into crumbs against his hand that wouldn't grasp.

For a second he looked really scared. "I can't."

I could see she was getting mad at him and that would only make it worse so I grabbed one of the magazines and whipped out the centerfold, T. Rantula right before the concert, cool: "Hey, baby, nosh on this."

"Futch!"

Tig was grinning. "Oh Doctor, thank heaven you've come."

By that time even Welles could see what she'd been doing and she got all embarrassed and ate six of the cookies because she couldn't stop herself and then I had a lot and Tig made himself take one and put it on his night table, I could see he didn't really want to touch it and I could see at least half the things Welles was thinking, I was scared she might cry but by that time I was blathering about some of the kids in my section at school: Fangs Faraci and Teeny Hood that blew her nose on toilet paper and chewed it up and kept it in her desk. Welles and her folks had been to Farter's father's wedding in June, right up to the last minute Farter's mother was making phone calls from Maryland and New Jersey and Connecticut and she got as close as the Bee-line Motel, maybe she would have a shotgun, blood shed on the wedding cake, hers or Mr. Fisk's; whatever it was she had planned Mrs. Welles went over and talked her out of it. Then Welles and I got going on Farter's father's girlfriend's trousseau, the maternabikini and the preg-pouch wedding dress, we were going up, trying to take Tig with us, he was looking pink and snorting, after a while we were laughing and spraying crumbs all over his bedspread, which he noticed finally and had to brush off, so we hadn't really taken him anywhere or done anything with him, we were all back where we started.

Welles said, "So what should we tell them over at the school?"

Tig said, "Tell them to save me a space in the smartass section."

"When till, the twelfth of never?"

Tig said, "Oh, I'll be back any minute."

She got hopeful. "You're going off your diet?"

"Oh no, I can't." His eyes were so clear I could see right through them, there was nothing behind. "I don't really have to."

"They're never going to let you out if you don't get better."

"There's nothing the matter with me," Tig said. "I'm fine."

"But you've got all that stuff going into your arm."

"I don't need that, I never did need it." For a minute he looked as if he would start ripping the tape off and taking the needles out, but all he did was touch them and then look up at us with his chin up and his eyes shining. "All I have to do is convince them and they'll have to let me go."

"Oh Tig."

I guess Welles was trying to, you know, motivate him. She was so practical. "They're never going to take you on the track team if you weigh twelve pounds."

He was, what: stoned on starving? "The track team?"

"That you were going out for, remember?"

He shook his head as if he didn't.

I was struck with an early picture of him running, losing weight to build up speed; he wanted to be a race-track dog, stripped down.

"You were going to make the team."

Then even I got mad. "Then why the hell did you start all this?"

And he came back from wherever he had been wandering and said, "Oh, this," as if it was nothing, so simple. "To get it under control."

"Tig!"

"Don't you see?"

He looked so sunny and hopeful that I wanted to hit him: fighting dragons with a plastic sword. "Tig, dammit."

So it was Welles that pulled me back this time, she said there was a concert in Boston that we all had to go to, we had to spend at least one weekend in the Framingham Mall and do everything, there were hundreds of movies we had missed, we had to take the day boat to Nantucket but we couldn't do anything until he got out of this damn hospital, right? Tig had to say, Right, and she said, Any way you can, so he said, Any way I can, I think he really planned to, but who knows?

She went to the bathroom so I was alone with him.

There was all that stuff we couldn't talk about, I couldn't explain. I said, "Do you want me to do anything?"

"Help me, Futch, OK?"

God I would do anything.

He was looking furtive, I thought maybe it was all going to come out, could I handle it, and then he only said, "Eat my cookie before she comes back?"

"She'll know you didn't eat it."

"She can't prove it, it'll get her off my back, OK?"

"OK, Tig. OK." I looked at him and I thought I would do anything for him, eat vomit if that would help, so I took it and had a hard time getting it wet enough so I could swallow. Afterward I said, "Look, there's this thing I've been, I didn't know if. Oh hell, Tig. Is there anything I should have, I mean. Oh God, why did this happen?"

Then he looked down at his transparent arms and gave me this smile that freed me forever and said, "This? I did it, OK? Me."

Welles came back and it was time to go. Tig tried to keep us, he put on a new record we had to hear and we shuffled a little, bopping to the music, he got out of bed and pulled the rack over and more or less leaned on it so there were three of us dancing, and when that song was over he made us stay for another one, he was so tired by that time he could hardly stand up and Welles saw it, she said, "Tig, we've really got to go."

"Wait."

I said, "We'll be back."

"Look, why don't you take some of this stuff?" He was grabbing at things one-handed: candy, magazines.

"But that's for you."

"Oh come on, I want you to take it." A light went on behind his face, all the extras had been burned off so what you saw was pure Tig, shining. "I really do."

We ended up at the door with our arms full of his things, I was thinking, God, I don't know what I was thinking: too much. I said, "T."

He said, "Rantula."

Then the elevator came and that was the last we saw of him.

The stuff was too heavy for us so we stopped in the lobby and gave it to them to take up to pediatrics and then we went on outside into the September light, the trees were changing right in front of us and we ran for a while because we were so glad to be out of that place. I remember we had to hurry because the school year was leaving with or without us and we wanted to be on it because there were so many things beginning, if Tig couldn't come, we couldn't wait for him.

We talked about it all the way home: things we might do. Welles thought maybe if we stole him and hid him somewhere that his family couldn't find him, we might get him eating, she would cook and I would find new recipes and watch him eat. I got this picture of the two of us cracking open the hospital and lifting him out, with our fangs bared and all our black hairs gleaming but we couldn't

It wasn't

I said what if we got rid of Mr. Tilghman, we would whip into the satins with the black sequins and do our Armageddon number on his lifeless body but I was uncomfortable even saying it because I was afraid we couldn't

Because we weren't

We were never

We were only

No.

T. Rantula was still knocking inside me, there were black hairs prickling in my groin and in the soft places under my nails, but I knew nothing I could do was going to stop Tig, we couldn't, nobody could because whatever had begun it, whatever the thing was that had Tig, it was feeding on itself now, Tig was burning himself up from the inside out as fast as he could, he could hardly wait for it to be over and we couldn't stop or change that any more than we could stop each other changing as we watched.

At our corner we hugged for a minute, recognizing what was. Welles said:

"So I'll see you."

"Yeah, right."

Then she ran and I started down our street.

When I came in Pop asked me about Tig.

I didn't want to talk about it so what I said was, "He's OK."

What I meant was: you should have done something about Mr. Tilghman while there was still time, you should have done it before any of this could happen to us, but by that time I knew that killing Mr. Tilghman wouldn't do it, any more than Tig starving himself would put the things in his life back where they were before it started.

18.

THREE WEEKS LATER Welles was going steady with some jerk from the sophomore smart section who looked just like my cousin at Yale that I have always hated, you would never know she had even been to London, and the only time we saw each other was waiting for the bus. I had found some kids to hang out with, starting with Jackie Rasker, with Farter gone he had quit being a pain in the ass. We followed Arnie Moon for one solid week and finally got him to cry by sneaking last year's books into those covers he made out of wallpaper samples, which he didn't discover until we went in for the open book test in first-period French. The Tuccis got sent to VoAg to be mechanics but that left Vincent Garganza that they used to hang out with,

I always knew he was smart; there were a couple of faculty kids that had gone to parochial school up till this year, we got them and it rolled along like the tar-baby, picking up people, so school wasn't so bad. We went everywhere in a gang, when the first game of the season started we were packed into the bleachers, passing blackberry wine that Vin had brought and yelling a lot. One kid was this Diane, we ended up next to each other with everybody mashed around so you didn't know who was with who, the team was playing under the lights with thousands of bugs bashing themselves into the reflectors and everybody squished together and sweaty because it was only September; we all had to jump up and yell every time anything happened, a whole bunch of bananas jumping, locked together, except toward the end of the third quarter we came down again with my arm around her where it stayed all the way through the parking lot and into this kid's car that we went to Brigham's in, it was part learning what she felt like, just the edges, with the, God, complications, but the other part was just being *with*; they finally kicked us out for shooting straw covers and I was late getting home.

I could see the light was on which meant Pop was probably up and I would get in trouble but I didn't care, I had this quick picture of me in the boat in the middle of last summer, there it was floating in the middle of the St. John's River, but I was seeing it from so far off that all I could think was, that dumb kid, he was so far away I almost didn't know him.

I was already late but I had to stay in the street to watch the car vroom off with Vin's big brother gunning the motor and everybody yelling, I stood there letting the sweat cool and dry on me and I was thinking, yeah, right, real life, these can be my people. Then I went in and Pop didn't even notice I was late; he was waiting up to tell me about Tig. It didn't happen the way I had expected, no matter what Welles and I thought the story was it wasn't supposed to happen at all, they can almost always save those people, except that this mystery pneumonia knocked him over and dragged him off before they could even identify the bug. The doctors couldn't figure it out. I guess Pop couldn't either, his hair was greasy-looking and sticking up and his face was slick with, um, I guess it was sweat; he just kept standing there in the hall.

"Fred are you all right?"

"Huh? Oh. I'm fine."

"Fred?"

I don't know what he thought I was going to do. I don't know if he was waiting for me to cry or try and tear up the place or threaten to kill him or Mr. Tilghman, at which point he could hug me or help me to be quiet and we could get through this thing together. The trouble was, I didn't do any of those things; maybe I should have, for Pop, but I wasn't even surprised; I had known about Tig from the day we left him in the hospital.

"That poor boy."

I said, "It's all right, Pop. He got what he wanted."

"God."

Pop was grey and nervous, sick and shaky-looking because he had never even thought about Tig before, or any of it, but to me it wasn't scary or terrible; it wasn't even very sad because Tig left us a long time ago, the day he started running. To me it was just very quiet, and after everything, that seemed good.

Pop said the funeral was going to be Monday and I said OK. He said Tig's parents wanted all his friends to come and I said there were only Welles and me. He said I might not want to be there because of everything, I guess he meant Mr. Tilghman, and that we couldn't all three of us go, Mom with him and me, and I didn't say anything. He said I didn't have to go if I didn't want to, and I said it didn't make any difference. He asked did I want some coffee or something to eat or anything and I said thanks, no. He said did I want anything and I said no, was I all right, I was just fine, after which he finally said, maybe I would like to be alone? It took him long enough to catch on; he hadn't even asked about the game and there was no way I could tell him so I said I was kind of tired, if he didn't mind I was going to bed. I don't know what he was scared of or what he wanted me to do about it but whatever it was I couldn't, not then, all I wanted was to sleep.

I got up around noon. I heard him in the front room so I went out the back. I wanted to see Welles but their house was closed, she said later they had her off looking at boarding schools. When she turned out not to be there I went around to a lot of places that we used to be with Tig: the river, around town, our old school, the track. I stayed there a long time; I don't know, maybe I thought I would see Mrs. Estabrook and we could talk. I didn't feel bad or anything, I wasn't even thinking much at all, I was just going around.

The trouble was, the spit kept coming up in my mouth, I had to keep on swallowing and swallowing and after a while I thought maybe if I talked to Mom. I took a bus to the mall and when I got there I called the house from a phone booth but all I got was Angel.

"This is me, is my mother there?"

"Who?"

"You know. Fred." I still hated that name. "Is she there?"

"Not right now."

"Do you know when she's coming back?"

"Not really." Angel wanted me to hang up but when I didn't she said, "I'll tell you what, give me your number and I'll have her call when she gets back."

"I don't know where I'm going to be." I could feel the black hairs pushing through the skin on the backs of my hands.

"Well I don't know when she's coming back."

"Where did she go? I can call her there."

"I don't know where she went."

"But I have to talk to her."

Angel wanted to get me off the phone. "Why don't you call back later?"

"Well when?"

"Try in about an hour."

"Is she going to be there?"

"How the hell should I know? Just call back in an hour, OK?"

So I called back in an hour; this time the line was busy, I kept dialing and dialing and the line kept being busy, I was gettting too big for the phone booth, I was running out of air.

Finally they answered but it was only Angel.

"I'm sorry, she still isn't here."

"But you said she would be back in an hour."

"I said call back, I didn't say she would *be* back. Now will you hang up?"

"But I have to talk to my mother."

"Well you can't talk to your mother, she isn't here."

"Well if she isn't there where is she?"

Angel was getting mad at me. "How the hell am I supposed to know?"

She got me off by saying she thought she might be there by seven, why didn't I call back around then.

It was getting harder and harder to wait, I kept bumping around the mall, I went into all the stores so many times they were beginning to get suspicious and I was running out of things to do. I bumped into some kids from school which used up a little of the time but pretty soon they had to go home because it was getting dark; I knew Pop would be expecting me, I ought to call at least, but I was running out of dimes and I couldn't go home until I talked to her. Maybe I could have gone down there but by that time I had used it all up on food and the phone and I only had a couple of dimes left; besides, whatever it was that I had to see about wasn't in Cambridge, it was here. I found an old newspaper and read it through twice and went outside and walked around the whole mall but when I looked at the clock again it still wasn't seven.

I called anyway.

"Is she there?"

"I told you to wait until seven."

"Doesn't anybody else ever answer the phone?"

"I'm waiting for a call, all right? Now, will you get off the line?"

"I just thought she might be back."

"Well she isn't. Now will you quit tying up the line?"

"Why isn't she?"

"How should I know? She has her own life, you know."

"She can't, she's my goddam mother."

I was yelling at her which is why she yelled back, right before she hung up: "Not any more."

The last days were filled with fire and death

I came out of the phone booth huge. The whole place shook with my eight-beat steps, if they had seen my face they would have screamed at the venom streaming, the blackness, the size.

And death and death and death and death

The spider was running out of words

The black thing said with its last breath

Had to do something

I got to be moving along

Crack him open and expose his guts, anything

These are the last days the last days the last

So I went to Tilghmans' house. I went in the cellar way, like always, I don't know what I was going to do but the day had moved along with no real changes, Tig was dead and nothing had changed, nobody was even crying, he had done all this and his father and mother were out in the car like always, dressed up to the hollow faces, he had died for nothing, fangs bulging and all that spit I had been swallowing had turned poison, so I had to

Rantula, ta ta ta ta ta ta-

No backup this time, there was never any backup, but I was going to do it anyway, I had to

I don't know how I fit through their cellar door

I thought I was going to get him.

So there I was in their cellar, the car was gone, maybe they were both at the funeral home or else he had dropped her and then went off to buy another pair of English boots, and I was in their cellar fuming, T. Rantula lying in wait, if I had been given time maybe I could have figured out what to do about it, found some way to kill him or get the police on him but as it was I just got there, I was standing down there looking at all of Tig's stuffed animals lopping over and all the dusty broken toys we had never really liked and there was the Ping-Pong table over near the wall with that plastic monster Space Walk sitting on top of it with the sun on crooked and the planets hanging off their rods, I didn't know what to do so I went looking for Tig's hunting knife, I don't know what I thought I was going to mess up but I had to mess up, maybe I could even stab the bastard, rantula memorial to Tig, but I didn't have time to think about it because the house turned out not to be empty after all, the upstairs door from the kitchen opened and there was his father staring at me from the stairs.

"Who's that?"

T. T. Rantula.

"What are you doing here?"

"Tig's dead."

"You don't have to tell me." He came down the stairs with the right kind of face for somebody that their kid has died. Did he feel anything? "What are you doing here?"

"Nothing."

"Why didn't you come to the front door?"

"I don't know."

"Why did you come?"

He was closing in and I started backing. I hadn't found the knife, would never find it. I was trying to think of what to say, I backed behind the Ping-Pong table and

when I had him on the other side I said, "Tig said I
could have some of his toys." It was all I could think of
to tell him.

"My son is dead and all you can think about is his
toys?"

"I can't think about anything, Mr. Tilghman, OK?"

He was moving around the table, he had his hand out,
I didn't know if we were supposed to shake or what, he
said, "Look, Freddy."

These are the last days the last days the last . . .

"Don't call me that."

He was still moving in, all that behind us and he was
still so smooth. "I think you'd better go home now."

It's gotta be the end because it's worse than the past.

I backed into the wall, I don't know what I thought he
was going to do, rape me? "Go away."

"You'd better go home now, son, you're upset." His
face was just as smooth as ever, he was only frowning a
little, as if he was concentrating, but he was getting
closer and closer, great big scary bastard, and I didn't
know what to do about it, all my poison spit was building up and so I yelled.

"Don't touch me."

"I was just."

"Don't touch me, it's all your fault."

"You don't mean that."

"Don't come near me." I grabbed something to protect myself: one of the planets. "Faggot."

"What did you say?"

I said, "Faggot," and I threw it and hit him in the
head.

"Why you dirty little creep."

T. Rantula and me were on our eight legs now, dripping spit and yelling, "Faggot, it's all your fault."

I got off two more before he closed in on me, a planet and the capsule, I think, I was grabbing for the sun, maybe I thought I could brain him with it and it would all be over; I was screaming and his whole outside had cracked open at last and let out all the ugliness, he was raging at me, hissing through his teeth:

"Don't—" he had me

"Faggot."

"You—" he was shaking me

"Faggot."

"Ever—" something banging, what?

"Faggot."

By that time I could hardly hear myself because of the thunder in my head, he had grabbed me by the shoulders the second I started yelling and all the time he was saying that and I was screaming that he was shaking me, faggot, faggot, faggot, three bashes that sent the back of my head against their brick basement wall, he didn't even see me, he was just shaking and bashing and where was T. Rantula?

The last days were filled with fire and death

Probably the blood came from my nose. I don't know if I went out for a second or not I don't think so, I lost track, all I know is there was blood and we both heard this voice quavering from the top of the stairs, faroff and sweet: "Honey, is that you down there?"

The big thing sinking into death

He was right in the middle and he stopped cold. "Maida?"

"I thought I heard something."

The spider said with its last breath
He just let go.

"It's nothing, dear, I'll be right up."

His face went back just as if it had never even happened. So I hadn't hurt him, the truth hadn't hurt him, T. Rantula went out to get him and it didn't make any difference, nothing made any difference.

I gotta be moving along.
I couldn't do anything.

So I had come to his house to try and pay back for Tig, to do something, and I couldn't do anything because I was never T. Rantula, I was only Futch that was already starting to cry just like a little kid.

He didn't pay any attention, he just got me up through the cellar door and out on their walk, and when I didn't fall over he gave me a hard push and said, "Go home."

There I was in the cold night just a stupid kid that I did the only thing I could do, I tried to stop crying and I went home. Pop was at the door almost before I got there, I guess I should have called him before from the mall, he was wild, and when I more or less fell in the door he grabbed me, he started hugging me and wouldn't stop. Then he saw the rest of me and he said, "My God, what happened?"

But I wouldn't tell him, there was just too much and I couldn't stop crying.

"Fred, are you all right?"

All I said was, "Oh Daddy," and let him take care of it.

He looked at me for less than a second and said, "Get in the car."

We went in without even knocking. While he was down there in the front hall trying to get Al into a fight

I went up and found her in her room. When she saw me she gave me a big hug without saying anything and after she rocked me for a minute she went over to the corner basin and wet a washcloth and started on my face.

"What happened?"

"Tig's dead."

"Oh Freddy. Poor Maida."

Poor Tig. "The funeral's tomorrow."

"Poor baby."

"Mom."

"What do you want me to do?"

"I want you back."

"You know it wouldn't be the same."

"I don't care if it isn't the same, I need you right now."

"Oh Freddy."

"Dammit, Nina." There was Pop clumping in. "Get your things."

"Wait a minute, Ted." She was looking at me. "Freddy?"

"Just for a while. The funeral's tomorrow."

"Ted, I don't know if I . . ."

Pop's face was sort of clogged. He said, "You know damn well I wouldn't ask you for myself."

She had been looking at me but she turned to him, she was blazing. "You know damn well I wouldn't do it for you."

"Your son needs you, Nina."

"Would you mind waiting downstairs?"

When he had finally gone she turned around and took me by the shoulders, the same places Mr. Tilghman had grabbed me but this was Mom's touch that could make you well. "Freddy?"

"Please Mom."

She tried to smile, God she was weary, she was crying too. "You know I'm coming because you need me now, and not for any other thing."

"Yes Mom."

"And you understand why I can't stay."

"You're never going to make me understand."

"No, I never can." She was trying not to cry. "But you know I can't stay."

I wanted to go for more but I saw how tired she was and I knew I was going to have to settle so I said, "Yes Mom, I know."

"At least I don't think I can." She was saying, for both of us, "It will never be the same, OK?"

I didn't care, I had her right then, I would have her when I needed her. I just let her hug me and said, into her shoulder, "OK, Mom, OK."

Pop was waiting in the front hall. She said to me, as we were going down the stairs, "The thing is, we have to know that and love each other anyway."

So there it was. After all that hard time there it was, I would have to go with it, we both would because it was what we had: we would love each other anyway.

I must have zonked out in the car. I remember them getting me out at home and I think I remember Pop walking me up to my room but I don't remember anything after that until I woke up late the next morning and knew something in the house was different and when I went down to the kitchen the sun was coming in and she was there.

She was sitting in her place with this really sweet expression, her face looked smooth and round, I don't know if it was wet or glazed or she had taken something to keep her smiling even though she looked as if she had just gotten over something terrible, an operation, maybe, or the flu; when she looked at me her smile shook and when she picked up her spoon her hand shook, when I came over to her we just hugged again; she looked and smelled so sweet I wondered if it was really her. She was all dressed up for the funeral, lipstick and stockings and a sort of golden dress that I had never seen, she even had a matching veil; the table was fixed up too, somebody had set it with silver and mats and flowers in a dish, there was a plate with a glass of orange juice on it for me and another plate with my breakfast waiting on the counter, I don't know if Pop did it or it was her. There was a lot of sun coming in, blurring everything and more or less warming all of us, everything looked so *pretty;* when we got to the church even that was pretty, hundreds of white flowers and light coming in the stained glass windows, the whole morning was so pretty that I felt more or less OK about Tig when it was over and I almost didn't mind having to see his goddam father in the front row.

They had it at the Episcopal church which I didn't even know they belonged to. When we got there everybody except the Tilghmans was still out on the front steps, it was almost like any other party, which I think was part of it; everybody had decided you didn't wear black to a kid's funeral, they weren't even calling it a funeral, it was supposed to be a memorial service, and to look at them you would have thought we were at the president's bash that he gives to kick off the school year. We came up the walk and I could feel Mom clutching my wrist but she had to let go the next minute because Welles's mother saw us and came over to hug

her and pretty soon Jackie Rasker's mother was making
a fuss and then there was Mrs. Moon being holier than
thou, kissing Mom; after all the things I heard she had
been saying, I'm surprised her mouth didn't rot and fall
off; Mom started blushing and unfolding, she had even
let go of Pop by this time because everybody was
making so much fuss over her, you would think it was
Africa she had just come back from, instead of Harvard
Square. I could see some people whispering behind their
hands but Mom didn't notice and even I couldn't tell if
it was about how good or how bad she looked, I had
been with her through so many things that I couldn't
say how she looked at all; people kept coming up to
her and Pop and sweeping us along until the next thing I
knew we were all inside, more or less toward the back,
and I ended up on the aisle, confused, so that it was a
couple of minutes before I looked up and saw Tig there,
that was him in that box that was so thick with carna-
tions you couldn't even make out what it was, even that
was pretty and they were going to burn it later so it
would be clean. Things got quiet and I stood there looking at the flowers, trying to make out the casket underneath, thinking about Tig underneath the lid of the
casket, no not Tig, Tig's shell, and I thought God I am
going to miss him, I would have had to cry but it was
beginning so instead I got to sing, which I did, to keep
my mind off it, and while I sang I kept looking around,
taking in the crowd.

Everybody was there, Farter's father and his father's
girlfriend and even Farter all the way from Minnesota,
they had left the baby somewhere, and there were Mrs.
Fisk and her new husband on the other side of Farter,
so the row went girlfriend, I guess wife, on the end,

then Mr. Fisk then Farter then his mother so the three
of them were back together again, for the time being,
with her husband on the other end, he drives a semi
which I guess was her way of giving the finger to Mr.
Fisk; they were all dressed up to the eyeballs and looking really good together, for once everybody was
standing in the sun with their heads bowed, looking
nice, and I got this crazy picture of something like the
Easter parade, with the Tilghmans and all their relatives
up front, him forgiven for the day, and them followed
by the Fisks and the Welleses and Danny Abel's mother
and her lover, who was black, with Danny behind next
to his father and his father's lover who was foreign and
had on a tight suit; there were Patty Westover's parents
with Patty and her sister between them, trying not to
cry, and the Moons with Arnie and his ten dozen broth-
ers and sisters, the Raskers and Rich Oliver and his folks
and a lot of people I didn't know, everybody lined up
for once and facing in the same direction, even the three
of us, Mrs. Galitto had come and so had Mrs. Estabrook
who was crying for all of us and could not stop, we were
all there standing rank on rank almost like the saints of
God, shining in the dusty sunlight and dressed in our
best, all being as good as we looked for the time being,
at least as long as the funeral lasted, because we were
here to help each other get through this, more or less
praying for Tig; we were marching in place and if somebody slipped everybody else was there to shoulder in
and keep them standing the way Mr. Estabrook was
holding Mrs. Estabrook, the way Pop and I were hanging
on to Mom, we would keep on going along together,
either paying respects or trying to pray or saying the
same words as the pastor, doing all that either to help or

hide feeling: which, I couldn't honestly say. I could feel Mom vibrating next to me, she was like a trapped bird about to panic and bash against the cage and I had to push my shoulder hard against hers to help hold her down and keep her from flying out of there because she had come this far to help me and it was important for us to keep on going as we were for as long as we could manage it; she grabbed for my hand and I held on, I could feel Pop pulling hard on the other side, we were going to get her through.

So there we were together again at Tig's funeral, the three of us, Mom hanging on by her eyelashes and me not too sure we could keep her but glad anyway because she did love me, would love me no matter what, and Pop on the other side looking so damn pleased; I could feel her pulling and Pop trying to draw her, me leaning in, and I knew why we were all reaching, straining; all right, we were trying like hell to hold onto it: what we've already got.